Chef of Distinction!

Wispy Gorman

This edition published in Great Britain by

acorn book company

www.acornbook.co.uk

ISBN 978-0-9568628-1-5

British Library Cataloguing in Publication Data.
A catalogue record for this book is available from the British Library.

First published in 2012.

Illustrations by Staffan Gnosspelius © 2012
www.gnosspelius.com

Printed and bound in Great Britain by TJ International Ltd, Padstow, Cornwall

This book is dedicated
to those who fed me boiled cabbage as a child.

The world of an oyster

It all begins with the turn of the tide. That first barely perceptible swirl of the current that indicates the sea is receding. Moments later a new world is revealed. The rock pools are open to the sky and the gatherers, with their sharp knives, are crossing the sand...

Jasper was slurping an oyster from the sharp lip of its barnacled shell. The oyster, having just been subjected to a nerve-puckering squirt of lemon juice, found itself sliding down the red-darkness of his throat wondering: 'Now what?'

The life of an oyster is a pitiful one. A life of continual struggle the human mind would scarcely comprehend – gasping for sustenance in the swill and wash of the ocean's detritus, and all for what? – to be snatched up and flung on a bed of ice in some overpriced restaurant.

But not just any overpriced restaurant. For this was *Whittington's – the Premier Oyster Bar and Purveyor of Superior Fish* to those in the know.

And none were more in the know than Jasper Watson. Jasper had begun life as a small, under-nourished kitchen-boy. But he had risen through the ranks of white-hatted chefs and now had his own show, the ever-popular *Wats-on the Plate?* In fact, at this very moment, Jasper's assistants were busy preparing the kitchen where, later that same morning, he would be showing millions of listless viewers what they could do with a leg of lamb.

He washed down the oyster (which was by now more confused than ever) with a glass of his favourite chilled Vouvray. He picked up the wine glass and twirled it by its slender stem, the bubbles which had been clinging companionably to the side were wrenched free and rose to the surface where they burst and disappeared.

A few moments later, so had Jasper Watson.

*

Elsewhere, in another part of the same city, Dick Scabbit murmured and turned over, and went back to sleep. In the room where he slept, the sunlight came bright through the threadbare curtains. The window was open, and the curtains rippled in the breeze. And somewhere, on the far periphery of his consciousness, he heard the distant rumbling of traffic in the cool morning air – the sounds of a city stirring into wakefulness.

The Master at Work

Over in the television studio, Jasper was already hard at work.

'Hello and welcome to *Wats-on the Plate?* Well today I am going to show you how to prepare… Roast Lamb. But first, take a look at this.'

The camera drew closer. The cameraman beetling forward with his feet either side of his mobile perch.

'Now this,' said Jasper, flickering a razor-sharp knife at the lens, 'is *The Slicer!*' – there was a jolt as the camera darted backwards – 'One of my own specially designed cluster of knives, made for me by *Smilers of Sheffield.*'

He took a prime leg of lamb, scored the back of it with *The Slicer*, and rubbed salt into the wound.

'There,' he said, stepping back to admire his knife-work. 'Superb,' he said, modestly. 'And now for one of my own special touches: a sprig of rosemary! Look at that, eh? Straight off the bush. So fresh you can see the droplets of dew between its prickles!'

'O-hhh y-e-s,' murmured a disembodied voice somewhere behind the camera.

Even Jasper's most insignificant moments were shared with, commented on, and enthused over, by the Disembodied Voice. A voice whose gentle resonance and quiet wisdom was loved by all who heard it. Except for Jasper who had come to resent the interruptions.

'And I would serve this,' he continued, 'on a plate, with some garnish.'

'O-hhh? What kind of…'

'White – a white plate. Definitely a white plate. It sets off the tones of the lamb. And the rosemary.'

He fussed around with the rosemary. Laying it lengthwise, crossways. Then stepped back and looked at it critically, as if lost in deep thought.

Michelangelo coming down the ladder after completing the Sistine Chapel, Leonardo stepping back from the Mona Lisa. And now Jasper and his plate of lamb. All felt much the same thing: it was done. But not quite. Or maybe it was. He adjusted the rosemary a fraction to the left.

'That's what it's all about, you see – attention to detail. That is what elevates a simple meal, no matter how humble or slightly burnt even, to the level of a work of art.'

There was a stifled yawn. 'And of course this is where you come in,' said the Voice.

'Precisely,' said Jasper. 'Although in essence this is something anyone can do. Well, not anyone obviously. I mean it takes a certain... Umm...'

'Panache?' said the Disembodied Voice. 'Well anyway, is that all we've got time for?' he asked hopefully.

'What?? Oh no, not yet!' snapped Jasper. 'We've got the *Chef of Distinction!* to do yet.'

'Ah yes,' said the Voice, 'The *Chef of Distinction!* How could I possibly forget?'

The *Chef of Distinction!* was an annual competition, sponsored by *Smilers of Sheffield*, in which Jasper and his camera crew scoured restaurants, hotels and wine-bars in search of the finest chefs in the land. One of whom was then crowned with the accolade *Chef of Distinction!* while the rest were branded as also-rans and left smiling dejectedly at the camera, before returning to a lifetime of obscurity and catering for coach-parties.

The lucky winner, however, was elevated to another realm entirely. They were presented with a *Smilers' Slicer* with a gold-plated hilt, a nice red sash, and a framed certificate with their name in fancy writing.

'So next week,' said Jasper, having told the viewers all about *The Slicer*, the certificate, and the sheer excitement of trailing round kitchens, 'next week we begin our search for the *Chef of Distinction!*'

He sighed and looked down at the lamb.

It had been a tough morning for both of them.

Mickey Jakes makes a speech

Mickey Jakes was expanding. He had been for years. He stood in front of the bathroom mirror, one side of his face lathered in white shaving foam, his razor poised.

'I have a proposal for you boys,' he said, waving his razor. What he needed was an opening. A good beginning that would set the tone and grab their attention.

'I…'

'Have you finished in there yet?' said his wife Mandy who was standing outside the door in orange carpet slippers and a dressing gown with sunflowers all over it.

'Yes love, just coming. Just finishing off now.'

Mickey Jakes makes a speech (Part II)

'Gentlemen, you are among my oldest, and most loyal customers…' Mickey Jakes opened his arms expansively and looked at them each in turn: the tall, lean figure of Harry Hop-Pole, in his customary red baseball cap; the short, wiry figure of Babbings, his eyes looking sideways at nothing in particular; and Dick Scabbit, hands in the pockets of his long black coat. Only Scabbit was looking straight back at him, and he was frowning.

Mickey Jakes, proprietor and licensee of the *Dog and Bucket* was making a speech. It was not a very long speech but already the attention of his audience was wandering.

'Gentlemen,' he said again. 'You are among my oldest, and most loyal customers…'

By now they were really suspicious, Babbings shifted uneasily from one foot to the other. Harry scratched the back of his head.

'Do you want something?' asked Scabbit.

Mickey Jakes was taken aback. Or pretended to be.

'Want?' he said. 'Want? I don't want anything. Just the opposite. I have an offer, a proposal for you boys,' he said.

'What kind of proposal?' asked Babbings, warily.

This was not going the way Jakes had played it out before an interested bathroom mirror that very morning.

'Gentlemen,' he sighed, and puffed out his cheeks.

'I am expanding…'

They all nodded.

'Don't worry about it, guv,' said Babbings helpfully. 'I mean it's your build isn't it. I mean look at me – I'm as skinny as a whippet – which is ideal for my chosen profession, and you… well you're just the shape for yours. I mean if you was skinny, people would think the beer was no good wouldn't they?'

'My shape? What's my shape got to do with anything?'

The mirror had not responded in this way at all. In fact his shape had not even come into it.

He shook his head in exasperation and turned away. 'Come and have a look at this,' he said.

The Untamed World

Mickey Jakes lifted up the flap of the bar and led them out the back through what had once been the kitchen. A large blackened cooking range filled one wall, with a sort of pipe or flue heading up through the ceiling. A grey steel sink, a galvanised bucket, and a smelly old mop completed the furnishings. The place smelt of damp, limewash, and the mop.

'Er – hasn't been used for a while,' said Jakes.

He reached up and unbolted the back door. He rattled the handle, gave it a gentle shove. Then leant his not inconsiderable bulk against the door and eased it backwards, inch by inch.

'There,' he said, finally.

The door was open, and before them was a wall of impenetrable foliage. A tangle of briars and brambles, and head-high nettles. Above head-height in the case of Babbings.

It was as if they had taken a side door into a jungle.

'Always wondered what was out here,' said Harry.

'What *is* out there?' asked Babbings.

'Just a minute,' said Mickey, and taking up a large stick that was leaning conveniently beside the door, he led the way in to the undergrowth, slashing to left and to right of him.

It was heavy going. For Mickey Jakes. The others just stood there. Curious, but only mildly curious.

'Wish I'd brought my pint, now,' said Babbings.

After Jakes had hacked his way in a couple of yards he stopped and leant on the stick, panting heavily.

'Well,' he said. 'What do you think?'

It looked like the kind of place Hansel and Gretel would have been foolish to sleep in.

'What was it you wanted to show us exactly?' asked Harry.

'All of it,' said Jakes, gesturing around him.

'All of it? But that could take ages!'

'It doesn't have to be completely clear – I just want to give you the picture.'

'We get the picture,' said Scabbit.

'Remember it's potential we're talking about here,' said Jakes. 'Not what is. But what could be.'

' – could be a lot of things,' observed Babbings. 'Anyway, what was this proposal?'

'Ah yes, the proposal.' For in his eagerness to show what could be... he had temporarily forgotten the proposal. 'Well boys, summer is almost upon us. And I was thinking to myself only the other night, as I lay in my bed, *The Rose* has a garden, *The Green Man* has a garden, why even *The Laughing Gnome* has a garden of its own. So why shouldn't 'The Old Dog' have a garden? Why shouldn't the loyal customers of the *Dog and Bucket* have a garden to sit in and enjoy their beer on a summer's day?'

'I thought we were the loyal customers?' asked Babbings, frowning.

'You are, you are!' he reassured him.

'Hmmm. So it would be our garden?'

'Well yes… in a manner of speaking. Here's the deal: you fix up the garden. It needs a little bit of work. Ahem.
I'll provide tables and chairs. You sell the food – hamburgers, kebabs, chips, whatever you like…'

'Pies?' asked Babbings.

'Yes, pies if you like,' he nodded.

'I do. I like pies,' said Babbings.

'Good, and whatever you make…'

'Except for fish pie – I'm not so keen on fish pie. But all the others, you know – steak and kidney, beef in ale, beef in cider, beef in… chicken – I like chicken pie, too.'

'Good, and…'

'Chicken and mushroom…'

'Yes, and whatever profit you make is yours. For the first year. After that we go halves.'

'That's the proposal?' asked Scabbit.

'That's the proposal,' nodded Jakes.

There now follows a period of quiet reflection

'Well anyway,' said Jakes. 'You think about it, and let me know. I'm not in any great hurry. After all, summer's still a little way off. I just thought I'd give the right of first refusal to my three most loyal customers!'

They tramped back inside and, after a minor tussle with the door, which was as reluctant to close as it had been to open, the three loyal customers withdrew to the far end of the bar to discuss this unusual proposal.

'So? What do we think?' asked Scabbit.

'I'm not sure,' said Babbings. He had wedged his tool bag securely between the bar and the stool upon which he was sitting, and was now tapping his foot on the protruding hook of a crowbar. 'I mean what do we know about cooking, anyway?'

'Cooking?' said Scabbit. 'Why do we need to know about cooking? Anyone can slap a bit of meat on a plate…'

'Yeah, but you've still got to cook it first, haven't you? You can't just give someone a piece of raw meat, can you?'

'They do in some Japanese places,' interjected Harry, unhelpfully.

'But that's different.'

'How is it different?'

'Well, they do things differently there, don't they? It's a different culture, a different language, a different...'

'It was Clapham.'

Scabbit sighed.

Mickey Jakes, who had just finished serving another eager customer, was now wiping down the dark-polished wood of the bar with an old beer-towel. He made his way down towards their end of the bar, wiping vigorously, but quite unnecessarily, since not a drop of beer had ever been spilt there.

'Alright lads?' he said with a jovial grin, all the while the filthy wet rag going back and forth, back and forth, on the black-polished oak.

'Alright Mickey, just discussing your proposal,' said Scabbit.

'That's it. You boys discuss away. Like I said – I'm in no hurry,' and he folded his arms and looked up at the clock.

For a while the three of them drank in companionable silence.

'Well, Harry? What about you? What do you think?' asked Scabbit.

Harry Hop-Pole tipped back his head and yawned. 'I think…' he yawned again. 'We might as well do as he says, and sleep on it.'

Everything looks brighter in the morning

The sun had scarcely risen when Dick Scabbit drew back the curtains.

'Good morning world!' he said.

The sky was pale-pink over the rooftops, there was dew on the grass, and the air was still. Scabbit slid up the window and took a deep breath of the morning freshness.

And there in the cool morning air – was a swallow. The first swallow of the summer! Scabbit watched entranced as it looped and fluttered, dipped, slicing through the air and flittering its wings. Scabbit, who loved all forms of wildlife, took this as a sign, an omen. A summer full of promise lay ahead. A summer of sunlight and laughter. A summer of dreams and new beginnings. Of barbecue smoke, and raised glasses, and happy customers. He could see it all in his mind's eye.

The swallow had flown all the way from Africa to tell him this. And now, having attracted his attention, it was tired. It perched on a length of guttering on the house opposite, its wings drooping, its head on one side.

The swallow had flown all the way from Africa.
And now it was tired.

And together, they take up the challenge

Later that same day, three of the *Dog and Bucket*'s most loyal customers were back in their customary places. Mickey Jakes was not in evidence but Allsop the barman was presiding in his absence.

'Hey Allsop,' said Scabbit, and beckoned him down to their end of the bar.

Scabbit leant over the counter so as to be able to speak quietly.

'Now I don't know whether Mickey mentioned anything to you about this,' he said confidentially, 'but we are thinking of… entering into a form of partnership.'

'Is it about…' Allsop touched the side of his nose, 'the Garden?'

Scabbit nodded.

A prospective customer had walked up to the bar and was standing expectantly in front of the three gleaming taps.

'What garden?'

'Be with you in a minute, mate,' said Allsop. 'Just going to let these gents out the back.

There you go,' he said lifting up the flap. 'Come on through. And you too, Mr Babbings?'

'I didn't know there was a garden out there?' said the newcomer.

'Oh, yes,' said Allsop. 'Well there isn't yet. But there will be soon. Isn't that right, gents?'

'That's funny,' said the newcomer. 'You know I was saying to myself only the other day, *The Rose* has a garden, *The Green Man* has a garden, even *The Laughing Gnome* has a garden…'

They went through the kitchen and Scabbit slid back the bolt of the door.

He took a step back and then shoulder-barged it.

'There's another bolt at the bottom,' said Harry helpfully.

Scabbit drew back the bolt, put his shoulder to the door again and grunted as it swung open.

'Well that seemed to open easier than last night,' he said.

'The hinges have been oiled,' said Babbings. 'Look, that's fresh that is.' And he pointed to the incriminating dark stains beneath the hinges.

Something else had changed, too. The swathe Mickey Jakes had cut through the brambles was still there, although one or two clumps of couch grass had only feigned submission and had now sprung back into place. But essentially, the track into the brambles was as he had left it. As was the stick with which he had done it. But alongside it, leaning against the wall, were two others.

'That's funny,' said Harry.

'It is isn't it?' agreed Scabbit. 'It's almost as if he was expecting us to say yes.'

'But we haven't yet, have we?'

And without a word the three of them picked up their sticks and set to work. In different directions. Each pursuing his own path through the wilderness.

Scabbit swung the stick two-handed, hacking away at brambles, thistles, stinging nettles and any other piece of green living foliage that happened to be in his way. After an hour's back-breaking labour, the sweat was pouring from his forehead and his shirt was pasted to his back. But it was done. He had reached the fence that bordered the railway line. He rested on his stick, and looked around him. He sighed. The full magnitude of the task now became apparent. They would need help. Or some form of mechanical assistance. Perhaps both.

Scabbit turned and walked back along the path he had made. At one point it diverged. He elected to follow the wider path. The other was more in the nature of a tunnel, tall brambles arching over it and a voice, Babbings's voice, at the far end of it muttering expletives. At the end of the wider path, however, he found Harry who, with his customary economy of effort, was carving a tract through the undergrowth with wide sweeps of his stick.

'Alright, Scabbit? How did you get on?'

'I reached the fence,' he said. 'But it's no good. If only we had the right equipment… Where's Babbings, anyway?'

'I'm in here, aren't I?'

'Where?'

'Over here! Under this big prickly... Ouch! Get off of me!'

'I'm going for help,' said Scabbit.

Cross Bros army surplus, camping and outdoor supplies shop – proprietors: Joe and Jon Cross

Joe Cross was wearing a thick woollen army sweater with patches of cotton on the elbows and little hoops on the shoulders where he might be able to stick a cap, or a beret, or perhaps some useful item of kit. He was discussing torches with a customer.

'Now this one, if reversed, makes a pretty useful truncheon – if for example one was assailed in a dark alley. I mean if someone was foolish enough to assail *me* in a dark alley…'

And he tapped the heavy, rubber-covered barrel against the palm of his hand.

'But if you clocked someone with that…' said the customer.

'Exactly – they'd know they'd been hit wouldn't they? Or maybe not – depends where I hit'em. But then they shouldn't have been lurking around in a dark alley assailing an innocent, unarmed veteran of the Regiment, should they? They should have thought about that first, shouldn't they?'

'No I meant…'

'Hey! Who are you saying's in the wrong here?' said Joe Cross, leaning on the counter and brandishing the 'pretty useful truncheon' under the customer's nose.

At this point, Scabbit stepped out from behind the sheet of *Genuine Second World War Italian Army Tarpaulin – note reinforced ring-holes for lashing to truck or similar*, that covered the door.

'What do you want?' asked Joe Cross.

'I need something to hack my way out of long grass,' said Scabbit.

The would-be torch-purchaser slipped away unnoticed.

'What's the scenario? Have you parachuted in or what?'

'No, I got the bus.'

Joe Cross shook his head in frustration. 'No! No! – on your mission.'

'My mission?'

'Yeah. How did you get into this long grass?'

'Oh, I see what you mean.'

Joe Cross, all initial hostilities forgotten, was now leaning attentively across his counter.

'Well that doesn't really matter,' said Scabbit.

'Of course it bloody matters – you can't take a lawnmower on a parachute can you?'

'Well I – don't suppose it's ever been tried.'

'That's what you think, sonny.'

The conversation continued in this vein for some time before the floor upstairs creaked and footsteps were heard descending the stairs behind the counter. Boots appeared – black and brightly polished, then camouflage trousers (with big pockets at the knees), and down came Jon Cross, the other half of the Cross Bros partnership.

'What's the scenario?' he asked.

'Interesting one this,' said Joe. 'This operative,' and he nodded towards Scabbit, 'is stuck in long grass. Very secretive about his mission, too – won't give much away.'

'Long grass, eh. Good cover I suppose. What about supplies? Got any water? Purification tablets?'

'Look,' said Scabbit, 'I'm in this… scenario… with long grass all around me…'

Both brothers nodded, this was good.

'Just grass?'

Scabbit ran his fingers through his hair. 'No, as a matter of fact there's grass, stinging nettles, bindweed…'

'Ah, bindweed,' said Joe Cross.

'I'd say this is getting to you,' observed Jon Cross.

'Yes, you could say that,' agreed Scabbit.

'Hmmm. Well it's very important to stay calm. If you lose your cool and start getting all agitated that could jeopardise the whole mission.'

The voice of reason.

He stroked his chin, the bristles producing a rasping sound.

'Now, what you really need is a defoliant. I could probably get you something. But it might take a couple of weeks.'

'A couple of weeks??'

'Calm, remember. Stay calm,'

'I am calm. I'm perfectly calm. Give me a machete.'

'A machete?'

'Just a second,' he said, and turning to his brother, 'Joe if we might just confer…'

'Certainly, certainly. Good idea,' and the two of them withdrew behind a curtain of camouflage netting. Muttering ensued.

Scabbit sighed and looked around him. He walked over towards a rack of shelves containing *Assorted items – gas masks, ammunition belts, tent-pegs and camping spoons – various sizes.*

Scabbit picked up a large metal ladle. It was bent and pitted with rust. He was turning it over in his hands when a voice behind him said: 'That's no good – that's not what you need at all. Come with me.'

Joe Cross parted the camouflage netting and, with a last look back at the empty shop, Scabbit followed him through.

Behind the curtain was a twilit world that smelt of old canvas, and tarpaulin, and frayed and dusty rope. This was the inner sanctum.

'You're lucky,' said Joe Cross. 'Not everyone gets to see in here.'

Scabbit stumbled over a coil of rope.

They edged round an iron-framed camp bed. Someone had left a note on the yellowing canvas: *One Officer's Camp Bed, as used in the Western Desert. Note neatly folded blanket at the foot of the bed – remember it gets cold in the desert at night, but the stars are beautiful...*

In the next room there were sleeping bags hanging from the ceiling. They were suspended like dark pods, turning slowly on their threads like the delicacies in some spider's larder. Scabbit looked at one as he brushed past it. *Genuine Eskimo Sleeping Bag – made from congealed whale blubber, will withstand 39 degrees of frost. Last used in a centrally-heated flat after a party. 'Kept me toasty,' claimed the user. 'But I was pursued by cats for weeks afterwards .'**

'Wouldn't touch that if I were you,' said his guide.

Next they passed a large orange sack with the skull and crossbones motif on it, and a little scoop beside it. *Rat-poison! Help Yourself.*

'Wouldn't touch that either.'

---

*F.E. – 'pursued by cats' etc. – well you shouldn't have got Inuit! Hello and welcome! I am the Fastidious Editor (F.E. to you) and I shall be popping up now and again to lighten your journey through these pages. Incidentally, it is a fact not generally known that the Eskimos have over a thousand different words for sleeping bag. Incredible isn't it? Of course some of these are of rather obvious derivation like: bed-roll, or two-blankets-sewn-together… while others are more poetic: bug-bag… walrus-bag… snoring-pouch… bag of fleas… scratching sack... Mind you, I suppose if you spend half the year in an igloo you've got to do something to pass the time. Well, goodbye for now.

And finally, at the end of the labyrinth, they came to a wall in front of which Jon Cross was standing.

'Well, there it is up there,' he said.

Agricultural implement – one large, two-handled scythe (obsolete).

'Never thought we'd sell it, you know Joe.'

'I know, seems a shame, doesn't it? Old Grimes would be turning in his Grave if he knew.'

'Who's Old Grimes?' asked Scabbit.

'Well, we've been here 35 years now…'

'Thirty-five years! – makes you think, doesn't it Joe?'

'It does, Jon. We've been here 35 years now…'

'And before that, Old Grimes owned this shop…'

'I was going to say that!'

'Sorry Joe – you go ahead – you tell him.'

'No, no. It doesn't matter. You spoilt it anyway.'

'I said I'm sorry. Anyway he sold…'

'Agricultural implements!' said Joe quickly, and smiled smugly at his brother, who just shrugged, and sighed.

Old Father Time takes a bus.

Old Father Time takes a bus

It took the two of them some time to take down the scythe, and then to escort him through the tangle of camouflage netting and round the tarpaulin. But finally there he was, standing in a busy city street with a large rusty scythe over his shoulder. Scabbit smiled at a couple of passers by. But they just seemed to back away. He walked down to the bus stop, smiling to himself.

As he approached the bus stop the people waiting looked up, alarmed, and did their best to shuffle away from him. This was a good sign. People waiting, meant a bus was due along soon.

And then, at last it came. Cresting the top of the hill and beginning its lugubrious, third-gear-grinding descent was a bright red bus.

'About time too,' said a woman with three kids and four shopping bags. 'WAIT!' she shouted, as the bus glided in to a standstill. 'Let the other people on first,' she said. 'Not all of them – otherwise we'll be here all day. We were here before most of them anyway.' She stepped up to pay and opened her cavernous purse. 'And mind out for that looney in the big coat.'

'The looney in the big coat,' waited patiently till all were aboard and then stepped up into the bus.

'Oh my God – it's Old Father Time!' said the driver. He shook his head. 'Sorry mate, can't bring that thing on here.'

'Why not?' said Scabbit.

'Look mate, this is a public bus not some… audition for the Grim Reaper.'

This attracted a good deal of merriment from the other occupants of the lower deck, all of whom were now comfortably settled in their seats (with their bags on their knees and large items stowed carefully in the luggage racks provided).

'Anyway that could be used as an offensive weapon.'

'Not in a confined space it couldn't.'

'Get on with it!' said a voice from the back.

'Yeah! Make him walk like the rest of us!'

'You can't make me walk!' protested Scabbit. 'Not carrying this thing!'

The driver sighed. An endless, world-weary sigh through pursed lips.

'Alright then,' he said. 'Just this once. But don't ask me again. I'm doing this out of the kindness of my heart. It's strictly against regulations, and if an inspector was to try and get on now, I'd have to pull away in a hurry and pretend I hadn't seen him.'

'Thank you,' said Scabbit. 'Thank you very much.'

'Yeah, well you better stand here. And don't distract my attention while I'm driving.'

He pulled out into a stream of hooting traffic.

'So what's it all about?' said the driver.

'Long story,' said Scabbit.

'Thought it might be. Hey you haven't paid me yet!'

'You haven't asked me yet.'

'I was just going to.'

'So was I,' said Scabbit.

He withdrew a crumpled, high-denomination note from his coat pocket and offered it to the driver.

The driver turned to look at it, and shook his head. 'You are pushing it, mate. You know that?' He slid the note out of sight, and clattered out a few handfuls of change. Scabbit began scooping up the coins, balancing the scythe between the side of his head and his shoulder as he did so, and then dropping the change into the voluminous pocket of his coat.

'You know I had a feeling you were an odd customer when I saw you standing there,' said the driver. 'Anyone ever tell you, you look like Father Time?'

'No,' said Scabbit.

'Yeah, well you do. It's the scythe that does it. That and the long coat.'

The bus continued on its course, shouldering traffic aside and mounting the pavement as it rounded the corners.

As they passed the graveyard Scabbit dinged the bell.

'What did you do that for?'

'I want to get off.'

'Don't give a man much warning, do you?' said the driver, and he swerved across a couple of lanes of screeching traffic. 'Yeah? And what you hootin' about?' he looked disdainfully down through his side-window.

'Alright mate, mind how you go.'

The picnic in the clearing

Meanwhile, back in the garden of the *Dog and Bucket*, progress was being made. Harry had extricated Babbings, and the two of them had joined up their respective paths, like a couple of friendly badgers exploring each other's runs.

'You see I came along here, like this,' said Babbings proudly. 'And then that big prickly thing was in the way so I went under it, and then this other one grabbed me by the triffids!'

'Hellooo-ooh! Hellooo-ooh!' a piercing cry rent the air above them.

And looking upwards, they saw the blonde curls and smiling face of Mandy Jakes, wife of popular landlord Mickey Jakes, leaning out of an upstairs window.

'Are you making a maze?' she asked.

'Not intentionally,' said Harry.

'Oooh how exciting! I love mazes! We went in one when we went to the Isle of Wight for our honeymoon. Ahh,' she sighed, reminiscing, 'we had such fun! Mickey was lost in it for hours.

I sat on a balcony sipping a Martini watching him go round and round in circles. It was so funny. There was quite a crowd there in the end, all shouting directions helping him find his way out. No sense of direction, my Mickey, bless him. Aren't you boys hungry? You've been working ever so hard?'

'Not half,' said Babbings. 'Thirsty, too.'

'Well I tell you what – you have a little rest now, and I'll see what I can rustle up!'

And with that she withdrew, closing the window behind her.

'Ah, well,' said Babbings reluctantly laying down his stick, 'I suppose we better do as we're told.'

The two of them sat down in the pleasant sort of clearing they had created. Harry lay back with his hands behind his head, and his red baseball cap pulled down over his eyes. Above them the clouds were moving gracefully, puffy white clouds, drifting slowly, without a care in the world. Babbings closed his eyes, and soon the two of them were dozing peacefully.

'B-o-y-s? B-o-y-s? I've brought you a little something!'

Hers was certainly a voice that carried.

And out she came carrying a wicker basket.

'Oooh it is like a little maze out here, isn't it?' she said looking around her. 'Mickey would love it, you know. Such a shame he's got a Brewer's Meeting today, otherwise he'd love to be out here with you!'

'I bet he would,' said Babbings.

'Now I've just brought you a couple of things.'

'Ah, a pork pie!' said Babbings.

She spread a small blue-and-white gingham tablecloth on the ground and began setting out sandwiches of thick crusty bread, pork pies, pickled onions, a slab of cheese, jam tarts, even a bit of lettuce on the side.

And, most welcome of all, a jug of cold ale fresh from the cellar. An earthenware jug so fresh and cold it had broken into a sweat upon being carried up into the warm air and was now beaded profusely with little droplets of moisture.

A gentle swishing motion is what you're aiming at

When Scabbit arrived back at the *Dog and Bucket*, he was pleased to see that the little side-gate leading into the garden was no longer entangled with ivy, and the path itself was now clear and pleasant to walk upon. He strolled along it, the scythe digging uncomfortably into his shoulder. He found Harry and Babbings basking in their clearing amid the debris of their feast.

'Well, glad to see you two have been having a nice time,' he said.

'We have thanks, we've been having a great time,' said Babbings. 'Mandy brought us out some sandwiches. There might be some… oh, no that's finished too. Here, have a pickled onion.'

'Fancy a beer?' asked Harry, and he poured the dregs from the jug. 'Hmmm – thought there was more than that. Oh well. So how did you get on, anyway?'

'Pwwwwwww' said Scabbit. 'You don't want to know.'

'Fair enough.'

'Hey, you know what?' said Babbings. 'You look like Old Father Time!'

And he rolled sideways, convulsing with laughter. 'Old Father… '

*

After a quarter of a pint of warm, flat beer-slops, a jam tart and a pickled onion, Dick Scabbit stood up and belched.

'Right,' he said. 'Let's get back to work!'

'Oh, do we have to?' said Babbings.

'Look we're in this together, remember.'

'Hmmm. But we didn't actually…'

'Anyway, Chippie Monkton's coming.'

'Is he? I haven't seen Old Chippie for ages. What's he coming for?'

'To build the shed.'

'What shed?'

'The shed from which we are going to dispense food to the hungry crowd.'

'The hungry crowd, eh?' said Babbings getting to his feet. 'Don't want to disappoint the hungry crowd, do we?' He tucked in his shirt, rolled up his sleeves, and adjusted his braces. 'Right,' he said, spitting on his hands and rubbing them together. 'Show me how it's done, then.'

'OK,' said Scabbit. 'Now, what you're aiming at is a gentle swishing motion,' and he held the scythe, as if he was about to make 'a gentle swishing motion'. But didn't actually do so. 'It's easy really – once you get the hang of it.'

He passed the scythe to Babbings, who tottered slightly under its weight.

'Blimey! Heavy old thing, isn't it?' said Babbings. 'Not really my size. Here, Harry – you have a go.'

Harry took up his stance. He made a couple of preparatory passes, skimming the scythe over the grass.

'That's it! That's it! You're a natural, Harry!' said Scabbit.

'That's lucky,' said Babbings.

Harry began swinging the scythe in broad sweeps, while the others shouted encouragement.

'MISSED ONE THERE, HARRY!'

'BACK A BIT! BACK A BIT! THAT'S RIGHT – GOT IT!'

'You see,' said Scabbit. 'All we needed was the proper equipment. Sometimes there's just no point slaving away when what you need…'

'– is someone else to do it for you,' said Babbings. 'COME ON HARRY!' he shouted. 'YOU'RE DOING A GREAT JOB, MY SON! Look I tell you what,' he said, getting to his feet, 'if you're OK supervising Harry, I'll take these things back inside. Who knows, might even get a refill.'

'Good idea,' said Scabbit.

Three quarters of an hour later, it occurred to him that Babbings had been gone rather a long time…

Chippie Monkton

Babbings was returning from the bar with three pints of beer on a tray, and three more inside him, when a thin man in blue dungarees – with a ruler in his top pocket, and a red, carpenter's pencil behind his ear – pushed open the gate.

'Hello Chippie!'

'Hello Eric!' (For Chippie liked to be on first name terms with everybody, and had even succeeded in wheedling Babbings' first name out of him.)

'Here, got you a beer!' said Babbings on the spur of the moment.

'Oh, that's very kind of you. Don't mind if I do.'

And carrying their glasses, they walked up the path to where Scabbit was sitting.

'Hey Chippie!' said Scabbit getting to his feet.

The three of them chatted over their pints of ale, while in the background, the lone figure of Harry Hop-Pole went on swinging his scythe.

'Is that Harold, is it?' asked Chippie.

'That's right,' said Scabbit, 'he's a natural, you know. Just needed a couple of pointers and he was away. No stopping him now!'

'Has he done all this on his own?' asked Chippie.

'Ooo no!' said Babbings frowning in horror. 'We're working in shifts. It just happens to be Harry's turn at the moment.'

'Ah, I see,' said Chippie Monkton. He paused to take a good long draught of ale. 'So, tell me where you want this thing built then.'

'Well I was thinking somewhere over here,' said Scabbit. And together they paced the ground.

'Hmmmm,' said Chippie. 'Facing that way, presumably – with a nice view of the garden.'

'That's right,' said Scabbit.

Babbings, his opinion not having been sought, looked from one to the other, then nodded in agreement.

It was at this point that Harry looked up. He took off his cap and mopped his brow. He then became aware that he was the only one working, while his three friends were standing watching him, holding thirst-quenching pints of beer.

'Alright Harry!' said Scabbit. 'This is Chippie! You know Chippie – he's going to make the Shack.'

'The what?'

'The Shack,' he repeated. 'That's what we're going to call it: The Food Shack.'

'Is it?' said Harry. And laying down the scythe, he walked over to join them.

'Mmmmm,' said Chippie Monkton, pursing his lips. 'Hmmmm…'

For a while all that could be heard was the distant rumble of traffic, interlaced with birdsong. Then, faint at first, came the guttural, low-throttled growl of a single propellor-driven aircraft.* The others all looked up, their heads craning back to pinpoint the source of the sound, but not Chippie Monkton.

Chippie Monkton was thinking.

It was a slow process. Then suddenly, abruptly, his reverie came to an end and he announced: 'Yes, I can do that for you. You'll need three be two's for your cross-beams, ship-lap for the outside, four-inch posts… and you might want a bit of guttering just on the front there above the window.'

'Don't worry about the guttering,' said Babbings. 'I can get hold some of that for you.'

* F.E. – 'the guttural, low-throttled growl' – that would, of course, be the Mark V Supermarine Spitfire with it's distinctive Merlin Engine – 1470 horse-power, top-speed 378 mph (3 more than the ME109, ha!) Even faster in a dive! – say around 450 mph. Far better manoeuvrability, too. Effective range 470 miles, that's without the additional fuel tanks. And to think that over twenty thousand of these wonderful aircraft were produced yet sadly only a mere handful survive. Though quite what this one was doing flying over the garden of the Dog and Bucket that afternoon is anybody's guess. Now let's get back to the story.

'Six, twelve, twenty-four… forty-eight…' Chippie's gentle voice trailed off into meaningless mumblings, 'Two's? Three's maybe… just working out your nails,' he added in a brief aside to his riveted audience.

'Yes I can do that for you,' he said at last.

'How much?' said Scabbit.

Chippie frowned. By that one brief question, he had been reduced from an artist, a master-craftsman, to a man whose time could be bought by other men. His adam's apple bobbled in his throat. His downcast eyes took in his tattered boots, the bruised-green stems of slashed and trampled grass, and the boots of the men around him.

'I'd rather not accept payment,' he said with dignity.

'But we must give you something in return?' said Scabbit.

'I was just coming to that,' he said. 'In return… I'll pop in for a free burger whenever I'm passing.'

'Are you sure, Chippie?'

'You haven't tasted our burgers yet,' warned Harry.

'I'll chance it,' said Chippie, with a twinkle in his blue-grey eyes, ' – you only live once!'

So hands were shaken, and the deal was done.

'I like Old Chippie,' said Babbings, as his stooping frame was seen making his way along the path. He paused to close the gate behind him, raised a hand in farewell, and disappeared from view.

The Food Shack

Chippie Monkton was as good as his word. By dawn on the third day, the Shack was finished. It had a slightly ramshackle appearance, owing to the fact that it had largely been constructed from offcuts lying about in Chippie's yard, but the walls were upright and sturdy, the roof was sloped, and there was even a little black stovepipe through which smoke (a by-product of the cooking process) could be borne away on a passing breeze.

Chippie was just hammering in the final nails when Harry and Babbings came up the path, carrying a sign. A sign with the words *FOOD SHACK* painted upon it in black gloss paint.

'That's it,' said Scabbit. 'Lower it down carefully now.'

They did so. Then straightened up, rubbing their backs, theatrically.

'Right, now lift it up. Carefully now. Hang on a minute, we need a ladder for Babbings.'

'I don't need a ladder!' protested Babbings. 'Just help me up onto that box!'

The box was positioned, and the tottering Babbings climbed up onto it. Then, with only a little difficulty – minor grunts and groans from Babbings, a patient sigh from Harry – the sign was raised into place.

'Excellent!' said Scabbit. 'Fits perfectly!'

The three of them looked up at the sign.

The Food Shack was complete.

Nice job, nice job boys

It was a high-pitched, fractured whine and it was coming from behind the door.

'What's that noise?' asked Babbings.

'It's coming from the kitchen,' said Harry, nodding towards the back door of the pub.

'Jakes must be up to something.'

Jakes was up to something.

With a sudden ear-piercing screech, the iron teeth ripped through the timber – a line of jagged splinters flying back on either side. The blade withdrew. And came again. It seemed to be making for the door frame, sometimes dipping, sometimes rising as it tore its way through the shattered wood.

'What's happening?' asked Scabbit.

'Trouble with the lock?' suggested Harry.

'Bloody amateur!' said Babbings, shaking his head. 'Even an amateur could get that lock open. It's only an ordinary 'five-lever' and the springs in those old things…'

'OK, OK,' said Scabbit, because once Babbings got started on locks there was only one outcome.

The insatiable blade reached the doorframe, ripped a quick chunk out of it, and withdrew. On the other side of the door, the saw was laid down. The blade gave a last *ting!* and went on spinning, slowing down – till the blur of iron-teeth suddenly jerked into focus, and was still.

Jakes stepped back to admire his handiwork.

It was not a straight line, but the two sides fitted together perfectly – the lower half precisely matching the contours in the upper.

'Hello boys!' he said pushing open his newly-created stable door and standing in the doorway. 'I had a feeling you'd be out there watching me! Neat work, eh? See, the top half swings open, bottom half stays locked! Or, reversing the procedure – bottom-half stays open, top half swings… no hang on a minute, got that wrong.'

He went on demonstrating the door, opening and closing the two-halves. 'Clever eh? Now Allsop can stand behind this and serve the beer, whilst you boys serve the food!'

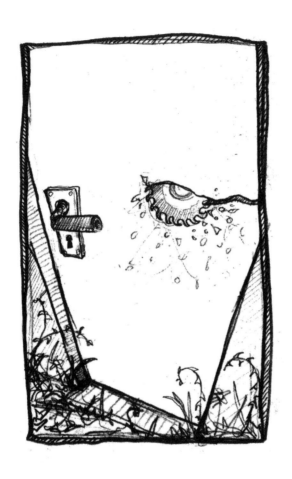

Mickey Jakes was up to something.

He strode through his new door and went over to inspect the Shack.

'Nice job, nice job boys!' he said nodding approvingly.

He stood for a while, hands on his wide, substantial hips.

The empire was expanding nicely.

But there was still much to be done.

'Well, no rest for the wicked,' he said, turning away.

' – wouldn't know,' said Babbings.

*

Jakes returned with a coil of plastic tubing over one arm. 'The tubes,' he explained. And began walking backwards as he paid them out, like a sapper laying a fuse.

'Now,' he said. 'We poke that one in there, like that. Connect this one up here, like that…'

There was now a direct conduit between the shattered back door, and a barrel of fine ale down in the depths of the cellar. Jakes ducked behind the counter and reappeared holding a large brass tap, which had a long and exquisitely-fashioned white porcelain handle. He clamped this into place, gritting his teeth as he gave the final twist of the screw.

'There! All done,' he said.

Mickey Jakes, who had once been just a humble barman himself, pulled back the tap. The interest of the three shed-dwellers was suddenly aroused. This was a sound they remembered. A faint gurgle somewhere far back in the pipes. Moments of impatient, bated breath. And then the froth-mottled ale gushed out into the bucket.

'Right, gentlemen,' he said. 'I think a toast to our new venture is in order!' and raising his froth-topped tankard, lovingly inscribed *To M.J. from M.J. in adoration*, he announced formally: 'To our new venture!'

'To our new…'

'…new venture!'

'Uh-huh,' nodded Babbings, his nose already in the pot.

Finishing Touches

At the entrance to the garden, a large banner proclaiming *WELCOME!* was raised unsteadily aloft, between two beanpoles.

'Up a bit. Up a bit. That's it!' said Scabbit. 'Hold it there!'

'Can't we tie it to something?' asked Harry.

'Yeah, I ain't holding this thing all day!' said Babbings.

'Don't worry! I've already thought of that,' said Scabbit. And with the aid of a four-pound lump hammer, he whacked a couple of tent pegs (supplied courtesy of Cross Bros.) into the ground on either side.

The lines were drawn tight. The pegs took the strain.

And the *WELCOME!* banner sagged in the lifeless breeze.

'Ah, yes! Looks nice that, doesn't it?'

The Grand Opening

The *WELCOME!* banner hung limp between its drooping poles, the fire was lit, the coals glowing and eager, and the inhabitants of the Food Shack were waiting for their first customer.

It was five seconds before midday – a pivotal time. The clock on the church tower of St. Anselm's wheezed and whirred and the ancient hammer swung down to strike the ancient bell. But before it could do so, the clock on the Town Hall brashly intervened: *CLANG! CLANG! CLANG-A-LANG! CLANG! CLANG! CLANG!* – drowning out the hallowed reverence with which the hours had been marked for centuries, back to when this was a rural hamlet with its own ploughman, lowing herd, etc.

As the last brash clanging began to fade away, the sombre reverence of St Anselm's church tower clock could now be heard: *B-O-N-G-G-G… B-O-N-G-G-G…* ringing out the hours as they were meant to be rung. Now here was a proper bell. A bell with an air of gravitas that somehow reminded the passer-by that he was not an island cut off from other men, with a once a week ferry service (crowded with day trippers who come bringing ice creams and litter and taking pictures) but a part of all things – an integral part, as indeed we all are.

B-O-N-G-G-G... it said again, just to emphasise the point. *B-O-N-G-G-G...*

It had been suggested that the Town Hall Clock had been deliberately set a few seconds fast to ensure that it always rang first. But this had been flatly denied: 'There is no mystery,' declared a Council Spokesperson. 'The Town Hall Clock is simply a modern timepiece. A superior modern timepiece.'

Although this explanation may have satisfied some people, the Weathercock remained indifferent, staring westwards with its tail-feathers projected disdainfully at the Town Hall. While below, in the yew-fringed silence of the churchyard, the great, and the good, and the others who'd got away with it, lay all higgledy-piggledy beneath their stone memorials. And the mosses and the lichens expanded ever so slightly, edging out over the tombstones...

It was now 12.01.

'Do you think anyone knows we're here?' asked Harry, pushing up the peak of his red baseball cap.

Eventually there was a creak as the little side-gate opened, and the sound of footsteps coming along the path.

The Weathercock
- with its tail-feathers projected disdainfully at the Town Hall.

'Quick someone's coming!' said Babbings.

'Who is it?' asked Scabbit excitedly.

'I don't know – can't see, the banner's in the way.'

'Quick get ready! Start smiling!'

'Shhhhhh!'

The footsteps drew closer. A shadow crossed the lawn in front of them. A long thin shadow. 'Morning gentlemen!' said a voice.

A sigh of disappointment.

'Mor-ning Chippie,' said the three in unison.

'I was just passing and I thought… I thought I'd pop in for a burger.'

'You're our first customer, Chippie,'

'I am? Oh?' and he leant on the counter, and smoothed the wood with the same strong, sensitive hands that had smoothed it with plane and adze, and grade F glass-paper.

'Nice to be first at something!' he said. 'Never did have much in the way of competitive spirit. Always seemed like a lot of unnecessary huffing and puffing to me. After all, we're all unique in our own special way. But still, it's nice to be first once in a while, even if it is only for a burger.'

'Well there you go,' said Scabbit handing it across. 'Our first burger!'

'Mmmm. Thank you very much!' said Chippie, and without further preamble he began chewing in rhythmic motion. 'Mmmm... not bad. Humf-fwargh-fwargh,' he said still chewing, 'Not bad, not bad. Surprisingly good in fact!'

The three chefs took the compliment lightly.

'Do you think it needs more pepper?' asked Scabbit

'No.'

'More salt, perhaps?'

'Er...no.'

'Onions?' asked Babbings.

'Onions...? Hmmm... Onions...? No, I wouldn't say so.'

'Good!' said Scabbit,

'Though if I was to be critical,' said Chippie, 'which as you know is not in my nature, but if I *was*, I would say that perhaps it does need a little something. But I'm not sure what,' he said shaking his head. 'Sorry, I can't help you there. Now if it was wood, well then I could tell you – in fact I did pick up a hint of oak and also beech in that charcoal you're using. But as to what makes a perfect burger – well for that you'd have to ask an expert.'

An Expert

Later that same afternoon, Harry had gone to the baker's to fetch more baps, while Scabbit was off on one of his unspecified errands, leaving Babbings in sole charge of the Food Shack. He had his head under the counter when he heard a cough above him. Not a real cough, but the kind of cough designed to attract someone's attention – in this case, his. He stood up. Leaning against the counter was a tall, smartly dressed man in a white-spotted blue silk tie.

'Her-humm,' he coughed again.

'Alright, heard you the first time,' said Babbings, who had an instinctive dislike of anyone suave.

'I am Geoff Ling of the F.W.U.'

'The eff double uu?' frowned Babbings.

'The F.W.U. The Food Writer's Union.'

'Oh, right. Hello Mr Fling.'

'Not Fling, Ling.'

'Fling-Ling? Can't I just call you Geoff? Anyway, what can I do for you?'

'I'd like a look at the menu if I may please.'

Babbings sighed, and reached under the counter. He handed him a large, red velvet-covered board about a foot long, with gold tassels dangling off the end of it.

Geoff Ling took it in his accomplished hands. Opening the covers he found inside a crisp, white sheet of paper with a single word scrawled across it.

BURGER.

Geoff Ling looked up enquiringly.

'– that's all we do. Burger.'

'Well, as I said, I'm from the F.W.U. and I thought I'd come along and have a free… er, taste one of your burgers.'

'Oh you did, did you?' said Babbings.

This was not the response Mr Ling had been expecting.

They eyed each other uneasily.

'So you won't be paying then?' asked Babbings.

'Well, naturally… no. But I shall endeavour to write something nice about you,' he said, looking around him, 'And your… er… establishment.'

'Hmmmm,' said Babbings.

Babbings looked Geoff Ling in the eye. It felt good to be looking a tall man in the eye. After all, the latter was not to know he was standing on a box.

'Listen, my tall friend,' he said. 'The problem is this: we can't just give 'em away, can we? Otherwise they'll all be wanting one. And then where will we be? I'll tell you where – slaving away in a shack in a field…' (rising to his theme) 'doling out free lunches to every Tom, Dick and Harry who happens to be passing. HI HARRY!' he called out.

'HI BABBINGS!' answered Harry, who happened to be passing.

Geoff Ling was getting hungry now, and was on the verge of laying down the empty white plate he was holding. But Babbings was a reasonable man.

'Look, I'll tell you what I'll do, mate,' he said. 'You sit down at that table over there…'

'Good man! I knew you'd come round in the end!'

'And write what it is you've come here to write. And then, when you've written it. I'll give you your burger. How's that?'

'But how can I write about food I haven't even tasted yet?'

Babbings raised an eyebrow.

For a moment it seemed the other had a point.

'Well if you didn't think it was so tasty you wouldn't be so keen on eating it, would you? Eh? And I'm sure an experienced gentleman like yourself wouldn't be fooled by his nose. I mean you can just smell those onions sizz-er-ling away. Sizzling. All sizzling and juicy. And then there's the burger. Ah the burger… Here have a whiff,' and picking up the pan he wafted it tantalisingly in front of his nose.

'OK! OK! I'll write! I'll write whatever you want!'

'Good.'

'But perhaps I could just have a tiny little taste? Please? Just by way of an appetiser.'

Babbings sighed.

So did Mr Ling, who by then knew he was beaten. 'Alright,' he said, ' – worth a try,' and reluctantly laying down his plate he went and sat down at one of the many vacant tables and took out his notebook.

*

A little later, when Dick Scabbit returned from his errand, ' – just had a few things to sort out,' he was gratified to see a customer, a real customer, hungrily devouring one of his burgers. The burger was so tasty, that the man, very smartly dressed and wearing an expensive-looking silk tie, was tearing at the bap with his teeth and swallowing ravenously. He was clearly a man who knew a good burger when he saw one.

'You see him over there?' said Babbings.

'Who – the only person in the garden?'

'Yeah, that's him – well he's in the eff double U, U,' said Babbings with a meaningful nod.

'Is he really? What's that, then?'

'The Food Writers' Union.'

'Ohhh…' murmured Scabbit, impressed.

'And this,' said Babbings, 'is what he wrote: *A fine succulent burger, grilled in a shed by experts. Kind, generous experts…*'

The morning dawned bright and clear

It was true they had not had that many paying customers, well none at all in fact, but they had attracted the interest of the press and, in these media-dominated times, that surely counted for something. So it was with a light heart and optimistic outlook that Dick Scabbit was undoing the shutters on this summer's morning. The shutters were a rather nifty piece of design on the part of the Food Shack's creator, Chippie Monkton. The bottom one folded down to make a sort of table, or ledge which was a convenient place to arrange plates, forks and serviettes, whilst the top one cunningly folded upwards to form a little canopy to shelter from the heat of the sun as it rose scorchingly towards midday. Scabbit hooked up the shutters, went back inside and lit the fire.

That done, he drew up a chair, one of three sturdy rustic efforts hammered together by Chippie Monkton from offcuts superfluous to requirements, and sat with his chin on his hands surveying the garden through the serving hatch.

It was a peaceful scene – the grasses wet with dew, the sun already exuding a gentle warmth, and the chairs arranged in pleasingly random clumps, as if recently abandoned by happy customers whose laughter still lingered in the air. Above it all, the sky had a blue that only a summer sky can manage – a sky full of promise of the good days to come, where the swallows flitted back and forth, gleefully consuming the less fortunate gnats, flies, and other winged insects who simply happened to be in the wrong place at the wrong time.

The Town Hall clock chimed 10 o'clock.

CLANG! CLANG! CLANG-A-LANG! CLANG! CLANG! CLANG! etc.

As its last brash, brassy note clanged out into silence, the bell of St Anselm's deigned to respond, its sedate: *B-O-N-G-G-G… B-O-N-G-G-G… B-O-N-G-G-G…* somewhat deadened by the droplets of summer dew that had settled upon its ancient surface.

And above, as alert as ever, the Weathercock was staring westwards, the morning sun glinting on its finely chiselled beak, its eyebrows arched in studied enquiry – for there on the horizon was a cloud, an unusually large cloud…

The Matriarch

Up in the clear blue sky, somewhere out over the Atlantic, the Matriarch was drifting along at her customary unhurried pace at the head of her herd. She had made the great trek many times before, and now, with a trail of other less experienced clouds behind her, she was returning.

The waves beneath her were gentle and blue, but darkened and became more subdued as her shadow passed over them. They were nearing land now, she could feel it in her water.

'Hey you two!' she called to two eager little cirrocumuli, who were getting ahead of themselves. 'Get back into line!' The chastened cloudlets wisped over her shoulder to their correct station, and the herd cruised on in stately formation.

The Matriarch gave a low grumble of satisfaction.

*

'Was that thunder?' asked Harry.

'Don't be silly,' said Scabbit.

The Storm Begins

Scabbit was staring out of the serving hatch at a patch of bare earth between two tufts of grass. Why that particular patch of earth had attracted his attention was hard to say. But it had. And once Scabbit's mind was focussed on something, it had a quality of tenacity about it. He stared fixedly at the spot. Behind him, in the darkness of the shed, Harry was counting baps: 'Sixty-seven… sixty-eight…' and Babbings was clattering pots and pans with a view to frying up some onions, when something extraordinary happened.

A raindrop splashed onto the very patch of earth Scabbit had been staring at, sending up a little puff of reddish dust…

'A raindrop!' he said, startled.

And a few seconds later, the cloudburst began in earnest. 'The first raindrop of the storm!' marvelled Scabbit, ' – and I saw it!' He drifted off into a trance, watching raindrop after raindrop splashing, bouncing, the green of the grass-blades flickering.

'*The parched earth it drinketh rain…*' he said to himself.

And indeed it was. The ground that only moments before had been cracked and dusty, was now suddenly awash with trickling rivulets, and tributaries of rivulets, all heading out, feeling their way across dry land. And the smell, the smell of the dry earth soaking up the life-giving rain. The scents of the dust, and the water. It was a smell that took him back to his childhood, and with a shudder he returned to the present.

'… one hundred and seventy-two…' said Harry, laying down another bap.

Then, with a jolt, the practical Scabbit came to the fore. He snapped out of his trance shouting: 'The chairs! The chairs!' and ran out into the rain, turning the chairs upside down so they would be dry for the customers to sit on later in the day.

Let's meet the Weatherman

'The foul weather is continuing!' said the Weatherman delightedly, and gestured sweepingly at the map behind him. The entire country was covered in black clouds from which sinister black raindrops were falling.

'Everywhere, you see! Here, here, and here… rain. Everywhere… rain!'

He sighed contentedly, grinning smugly at the camera. Then raised his eyebrows: 'And moving ahead to tomorrow…'

He paused and gestured back at the same map. 'More rain!' he said, slapping on a few more black clouds, just for good measure.

'So! A pretty bleak outlook everywhere!' he said. 'Glad I haven't booked my holiday over here! That's all I can say. Must be awful, you and the wife and the kids in the caravan… the rain drumming on the roof… mud everywhere… tempers fraying… arguments developing into major rows. And then back to work at the end of the fortnight! Ha! Tough eh?

We're going to the Seychelles in September.

It'll be sunny there alright!'

The effect of rain on the civilian population

The rain was still falling heavily when the side-gate opened, and Chippie Monkton made his way unhurriedly along the path. In due course, he arrived in front of the serving hatch.

'Morning Chippie,' said Scabbit.

'Morning Richard,' he nodded.

'Harold,' another nod.

'Morning Eric. I see you're on onion-duty today,' he said to the small figure in a flat-cap, who had his back to him.

'What? Oh yeah, morning Chippie.' He turned with a blackened, spattering pan and the smell of the onions mingled with the cold smell of the rain. 'Right, onions are done,' said Babbings.

'Bap,' said Harry, putting one on a plate, and opening it out.

'Burger,' said Scabbit, laying it on with the tongs.

'Onions,' said Babbings, heaping a few blackened shreds haphazardly on top.

Scabbit closed the lid, and one burger looking plump, charred and glistening with grease, was pushed through the hatch on a white paper plate. It was a seamless operation, efficient and well orchestrated.

But besides Chippie, there were no other customers that day, and it was with a feeling of disappointment, of disillusionment, that the coals were dowsed, the baps were put away, and the onions, in their crackling parchment outer shells, were left in their basket – spared the knife for another day.

*

Another day came. But there was no let up in the rain. Scabbit, having stoked the coals, was staring out of the serving hatch watching two sparrows taking a bath on top of one of the tables. They were clearly young birds, dipping their beaks, flinging a beakful of rain over their backs, and then waggling their tail-feathers from side to side. It was a futile exercise, since they could simply have stood still and taken a shower, but this was presumably more fun and they seemed to be enjoying it.

Babbings, on the other hand, seemed to be making an unnecessary clatter, banging the pots and pans about on the stove at the back of the shed. It was Harry, the sensitive Harry Hop-Pole, who first noticed that perhaps this was an outward expression of his friend's inner turmoil.

'You alright, Babbings?' he asked.

'No I ain't,' said Babbings. 'I'm fed up with this bloody rain!' He sighed and reached for an onion. 'Right, your turn,' he muttered, taking up a wickedly sharp knife. 'Anyway, what kind of nutcase is going to travel miles in the rain just to eat a burger cooked by three blokes in a shed?'

Jasper Watson demonstrates *The Fillet.*

'Now here's something they don't teach you at Chef School.'

He placed the onion on the chopping board, and then selected one of his knives from the extensive rack in front of him. His hand hovered momentarily over *The Slicer* before moving on to *The Fillet. The Fillet* it was then. He turned to face the camera, holding up the knife.

'And for this I will use *The Fillet* – one of my own specially designed cluster of knives, made for me by *Smilers of Sheffield. Established 1728. Nothing cuts like a Smiler.'*

He placed the blade carefully on the top of the onion. He tensed slightly. There was a sudden blurred drumming and for a while it seemed the onion was still whole – then it fell apart.

'You *do* do that rather well, you know,' said the Disembodied Voice.

'Thank you,' said Jasper, beaming at the camera.

The smile persisted, but the joy was beginning to wane.

Jasper was never happier than when demonstrating his own virtuosity with a sharp knife (a *Smiler*, naturally) but unfortunately for him, he now had other duties to perform.

The Search Continues

'Well this week we've come to *The Petit Chateau* to meet Head-Chef Monsieur Pierre Flamboyard.

Good morning, Monsieur Flamboyard. Or should I say: 'Bon-jaw!?"

A chef with a puffy white hat, a large grey moustache, and baggy check trousers stood awkwardly in front of the camera.

'It's not my real name,' he hissed. 'I don't speak French.'

'But surely everyone knows: 'Bon-jaw'? said Jasper. 'Bon-jaw! Bon-jaw!'

The grey moustache quivered, perhaps of its own accord.

'Bon-jaw.'

'Thank you Mr Flamboyard. Now what are you cooking for us today?'

'Wuzz-oh, a L'orange.

L'oronge,' he corrected himself.

Jasper sighed,* he had a feeling that M. Flamboyard was not destined to become *Chef of Distinction!*

*F.E. – *Jasper, of course, speaks French like a native – having served his apprenticeship under The Great Souffleur in his little bistro in the heart of the Latin Quarter. In fact it was he who awarded Jasper his Big White Hat. 'Magnificent!' said The Great Souffleur. (Magnifique!) Really suits you, that does. (Merci – said Jasper.)*

More foul weather on the way!

The map was covered in more of the sinister black clouds, and before it, in a truly alarming green-and-brown check jacket, stood the Weatherman.

'Well,' he said. 'No respite, as you can see,' and he waved a desultory hand vaguely in the direction of the map. 'No let up in the truly abysmal weather we've been having this summer – if you can call it summer! Just glad it's not my holiday, that's all I can say. We're going to the Seychelles in September – it'll be sunny there alright. Ha!' he smiled contentedly.

'Other than that… Well, no change really… just more of the same,' he held up another sheaf of black clouds that he hadn't even bothered putting on the map. 'These are spare,' he said, waving them in front of the camera. 'But I could put them on if I wanted to.'

St Anselm's Strikes First!

When it finally happened, it was so unexpected, that even the Weathercock was taken by surprise.

The ancient pendulum swung back and forth in measured silence. The ancient cogs, liberally coated with grease, clicked round, meshing perfectly in their hand-filed precision. There was a whirring click as the hammer drew back for the swing. There was a moment of complete, of utter silence… and then disbelief gave way to elation – the hammer swung down (nothing could stop it now!) and the timeless, resonant: *B-O-N-G-G-G… B-O-N-G-G-G… B-O-N-G-G-G…* rang out over the churchyard.

The rain dripped from the spiky yew, the moss crept a little further over the tombstones… and St. Anselm, who was buried in the crypt, turned over, and smiled in his tomb.

Peace had once again been restored. The hours were being rung out in the time-honoured way (rural hamlet, lowing-herd etc.) without the brash, recent intervention of the Town Hall Clock – the mechanism of which, a flimsy lightweight modern thing – had been affected by the incessant rain.

An Emotional Moment

The rain was now drifting in laconic waves across the front of the serving hatch. Chippie had come and gone, and the garden was once again deserted.

'Oh, well,' said Scabbit, as yet another day of rain drifted into a slow afternoon.

'Right, that's it!' said Babbings throwing down a cloth. 'I've had enough of this!' He paused with his hand on the door handle and looked round at his erstwhile companions, those same companions with whom he had shared so much, endured so much. In fact it was true to say that a bond had grown between them – a bond that anyone who wasn't there at the time, would simply never understand. He looked from one to the other. 'I'm going outside,' he said. 'I may be some time.'

It was an emotional moment.

'Alright,' said Scabbit. 'See you later!' And he turned back to the exciting game of draughts he was playing with Harry. The board was drawn on a sheet of cardboard, and the pieces improvised from beer bottle tops.

'Hmmm,' said Scabbit, considering his precarious position.

The door closed quietly, with a slight click of the latch that was all but drowned in the sound of the rain drumming on the roof, and splashing round about.

'Hope he's alright,' said Harry, hopping over three of Scabbit's bottle tops and sweeping them from the board.

'Oh, it'd take more than this to knock down old Babbings,' said Scabbit. 'I remember him that night in the Willesden Arena – back in his fighting days, taking on Old Pudgy Glubber – nasty bit of work he was, all clinches and head-butts and dirty tricks like that. One of Henderson's Mob he was – only reason he got away with it. But our Babbings soon took care of him alright, wouldn't let him come close, gave him a flurry of jabs and then his famous straight left, right on the cleft of his chin. Never knew what hit him. Next thing Glubber knows he's lying there, head back on the canvas with the stars going round his head.'

'Knocked out was he?' asked Harry.

'Knocked out? The bell knew more about it than he did! Oh yes, the cushions came in to the ring that night, alright! And there was Babbings throwing them back! I used to be his manager, you know.'

'What?' said Harry. 'You never told me that?'

'Oh, didn't I?'

But the glory days had gone, and the hero of the Willesden Arena was now walking sorrowfully along with his hands in his pockets, and his head bowed.

Poor Babbings made his way along the rain-glazed path. Even his closest friends did not understand his suffering, and then there was the rain... his slender hopes were slipping away. He decided to visit the bookies.

Babbings has a flutter

Babbings was a man of few vices, other than drink, gambling and theft. But on a day like this, there was only one that offered the solace his wounded soul required.

He made his way along the slick and darkened paving stones, opened the little side-gate and stepped out into the outside world. The rain was splashing down, and people were hurrying past with bowed heads and black umbrellas.

Babbings himself, spurned the use of a black umbrella, preferring instead to turn up his collar, hunch up his shoulders, and gain what protection he could from the flat cap on his head, which was soon a sodden mass, smelling strongly of the tweed from which it was made.

Darting from tree to tree, he made his way down the hill, alongside the yew hedge which bordered St Anselm's Churchyard, then he crossed over the street, passed the misted-up windows of the Café – a glimpse of blurred figures inside, obscured by the steam from the tea-urn – and arrived at the only shop without an awning in a road full of shops with awnings. The place stood out even in a downpour.

J.Hartless, Bookmaker – known variously as 'The Bookie' or 'That Bastard Hartless', depending on how things went.

His establishment was a shrine to vain hopes and shattered dreams, and very small pens. And everywhere those shattered dreams lay about the floor, torn into scraps or shreds, or some simply scrunched up into little balls and strewn about the place.

The air within was stale and lifeless, and the light was provided not by the wholesome rays of our very own sun (the central and pivotal point of our solar system) but by a few fluorescent tubes and the flickering TV screens which were banked up on the walls. The whole place was sealed-in, man-made and lifeless. And Babbings breathed it in appreciatively, the way a horse would snuff the morning dew.

'Right, what have we got?' he said, rubbing his hands together as he looked eagerly up at the board.

Epsom – Off.

Lingfield – Off.

Everything – Off.

'Hey Hartless! What *is* there to bet on?'

'Depends on the weather.'

'Hmmm? Now that might interest me,' said Babbings. 'What's the odds on this being the Wettest Summer ever?'

'What, the Wettest Summer Ever On Record?'

'Right,' said Babbings.

'Hang on a minute,' said Hartless and went back out behind his partition.

The partition was made from specially reinforced glass which had a metal grid somehow woven into it. And behind it, the rotund figure of *J.B. Hartless, Bookmaker*, could be seen pacing up and down. Up and down.

'You've got him worried now,' said a pallid-eyed regular* from the perch of his stool. It was a convenient position from which he could lean against a small red shelf, and view not only the entire bank of screens but also the front door at which his wife might appear at any moment. 'Look, he's pacing up and down. Means he's thinking. Can't sit still and think at the same time, see. That's how you know he's thinking.'

The blurred figure behind the partition stopped pacing and reappeared at the counter.

'I'll take it,' said Hartless.

F.E. – 'a pallid-eyed regular' – this is, of course, none other than Flapper Dooley, inveterate gambler and general chatterbox, who plays such a pivotal role in a later Scabbit adventure: The Ray of Truth.

Grasping the Gauntlet

Despite the unceasing rain and the occasional twinge of indigestion, Chippie Monkton remained faithful in his patronage of the Food Shack. Everyday he came and stood by the serving hatch, and ate his solitary meal.

'Raining again,' he observed, gesturing with a half-eaten burger. 'Mind you, it looks to me, as if it might be brightening up.'

'It can't be?' asked Babbings alarmed.

*

But sure enough, a few dreary hours later, the rain eased to a drizzle, and then finally stopped altogether.

'It's stopped raining!' said Harry.

'But it can't have!' said Babbings, running outside, with an onion in his hand.

High up, very high, were a flight of white birds, their wings beating slowly, against the grey-white sky.

'Ducks!' said Babbings, wonderingly. 'Hey wait a minute, they're not leaving are they?'

'Not ducks,' said Scabbit. 'They're geese – you can tell by the honk.'

'Oh yeah? – which bit's that then?'

And then, through a gap in the cloud came the Australians.

The Australians at 30,000 feet.

And then, through a gap in the cloud came the Australians…

The Australian Captain, known affectionately as 'Skip' to his men, was exercising his nimble brain by doing a crossword in the in-flight magazine. 'Four across…' he said, the pen poised in his stylish left-hand. 'Four across… The kind of nut you might find on the wing… Nut on the Wing… bird on the wing… Bird-nut?'

'Hey Skip! Ski-ip!'

'What?' he asked irritably, his train of thought in tatters.

'Hey Skip! Are we nearly there yet?'

'How do I know? I'm not the bleedin' Captain!'

'Yes you are Skip! Ha! ha! ha!'

'I meant the Plane Captain.'

He sighed, tapping his pen against his front teeth.

'Five across,' he murmured.

'Hey Skip! Ski-ip! Shorty threw an ice-cube at me!'

'No I didn't. It just bobbled out!'

'Always some excuse isn't there?' said the Captain.

'Not my fault – it was when we went through that turbulence back there.'

'Ooh! Ooh! Look out! Here she comes!'

The hostess was making her way rhythmically along the aisle.

'Alright?' said Shorty, hopefully.

She smiled professionally and fluttered her eyelashes in a 'you'll be lucky' sort of way, and made her way down to the window seat where The Captain was sitting.

'Hello, Captain!' she said. 'Not often we have two captains on board! Ah-ha-ha!'

It was the third time she'd made the same joke and they both knew the protocol by now.

He smiled, she laughed some more, another bright little cascade of it: 'Aha ha ha!

Well,' she said, pulling herself together. 'We'll be coming in to land soon-ish. At least according to his nibs we will,' and she jerked her head towards the front of the plane, where the other Captain was looking over the top of his dials at a very pretty cloud formation. 'So you might just want to tell your men…'

'Right, blazers on men,' he said smartly.

'O-oh! Do we have to?'

'Look we've been through this before,' said the Captain wearily.

'But – '

'I'll put you at Silly Point,' he said turning round in his seat.

'What's that out there, Skip?'

'How should I know?' and he looked out of the window at the line of rivets along the wing.

A very pretty cloud formation

High in the sky, where the weather was good, the clouds were taking a breather.

'Well done!' said the Matriarch. 'Some particularly good work there over Dymchurch!'

An old thunderhead-nimbus nodded at the recognition.

'One final push,' said the Matriarch and, as her clouds swirled around her, she exhorted them on to ever greater and better things.

They have arrived!

'Well now we go live to the airport, where I understand The Australian Touring Team has just arrived, is that right?'

'Yes!' said the Reporter on the Spot. 'Here they are getting out of their plane...led, of course by their stylish left-handed Captain... and here they are coming down their ladder... with their blazers on... very smart indeed.'

After a few brief words from the English Captain, who'd come all the way by bus from Ealing, the microphone was shoved under the nose of a man who had just made a six-thousand mile journey and hadn't slept for 96 hours.

'G'day,' he said.

'And how do you feel?'

' – knackered.'

'Perhaps you'd like to say a few words?'

'Perhaps I would,' and he put down a bag from which the handle of a cricket bat was protruding.

'Yeah, well it's really great to see the Pommies again. Very kind of them to come and meet us at the airport. And we're really looking forward to the upcoming Test Series.

Right where's my luggage?'

'Skip! Sk-i-ip!'

' – just shut up and follow me!'

'A man of few words there. The Australian Captain. And now, back to the studio.'

The Beginning of Summer!

Back in the studio they had found something to be happy about.

'Well, as I always say: 'When the Tourists arrive – that is the beginning of summer!'

'Not if you live in a ski resort it isn't.'

'Hadn't thought about that.'

'Anyway, what about the first swallow?'

'First swallow of what? Oh, I see what you mean. But surely that's just an old wives' tale.'

'Old wives' tale?'

*

The First Swallow was fed up. He was drenched and bedraggled. But he was not alone. There were now several other swallows perched beside him on the guttering, all waiting disconsolately for the weather to clear.

He shook his head, flinging off a scatter of raindrops. 'Look at me!' he said to a fellow bird. The bird in question, inclined his beak in The First Swallow's direction.

'Look at me! I fly all this way, and at the end of it, what happens?' The sharp-beaked companion opened its beak to reply, but The First Swallow was in no mood to be interrupted, 'I'll tell you what happens. It's rained every blinking day!'

'When d'you get here, then?'

'Eh? I was the first one here, mate – First Swallow, me.'

'What happened to 'Old What's His Name'? I thought he was always First Swallow?'

'Not anymore.'

'No?'

'Nah, got taken out by a cat on a wall in Andalucia.'

'You'd have thought he'd be too old to fall for a trick like that.'

'Yeah, well – old cat wasn't it.'

A little snack before lunch

The rain had slowed to a ceaseless, dispiriting drizzle. And it was against this background of softly falling rain, that the back door was opened (both upper and lower portions) and out into the garden came a singular procession. At the front, with a blue plastic scarf over her head, came Mandy Jakes. She was carrying a wicker basket tucked round neatly with a red-and-white checked tablecloth (that same wicker basket which had proved so welcome on a previous occasion). Behind her came Allsop the barman carrying a blue and white china jug filled with custard. And behind him, bringing up the rear, came Mickey Jakes himself, the landlord of the *Dog and Bucket*. Jakes was carrying a jug of dark frothing ale freshly drawn from the cask – though not filled quite to the brim. And as they walked, the raindrops landed in the froth, and dented it, as he had known they would. He had been accused, wrongly of course, of watering down his beer on previous occasions. But never had he done it so openly, so brazenly, and with such a perfect excuse!

They made their way carefully along the duckboard-path, a rescue party bringing succour to a beleaguered outpost. And it was not long before the ever-vigilant occupants of the outpost spotted them.

'Hey, wake up! We've got visitors,' said Harry.

'Hellooo-ooh! Hellooo-ooh boys!' came the piercing cry from the rescue party. 'Just brought you a few goodies – just a little snack before lunch.'

'Come in! Come in! Come inside,' said Scabbit holding the shed door open invitingly. 'Here, sit on this uncomfortable old box.'

'Ah, that is so sweet of you, Mr Scabbit,' said Mandy setting down her burden, and handing the picnic-basket to Harry.

'Have a paper plate. Can I get you a burger?'

'Ooh no thank you, but do help yourselves. Now in here you'll find…' and she drew back the red-and-white checked cloth to reveal pork pies, pâtés, a clutch of Scotch Eggs, crusty white bread, a slab of Mature Cheddar Cheese, a leg of ham with golden-yellow breadcrumbs encrusting the white layer of fat, and a jar of assorted pickles.

'Not sure what you'll find in there. I threw that in just as I was leaving.'

'That's alright,' said Babbings. 'I like onions. Well, used to.'

'Mickey! Come inside out of the rain!' she said, effortlessly projecting her voice. 'Mickey's brought you something, too. Go on Mickey, show them what you've brought!'

Mickey Jakes stepped forward and, bashfully for a landlord, he set down the jug of fine ale with the rain-pocked froth.

'I've been trying to shield it as best I could boys…' he shook his head. 'But with this rain – not easy.'

'Could be the way you were holding it under the gutter like that!' said Scabbit. 'Just kidding! Doubt we'll taste the difference!'

Mandy shrieked with laughter, chuckling, rippling like a jelly.

'Oh you are a one Dick Scabbit! Isn't he a one, Mickey?'

'He's a one alright,' replied Mickey.

'Fancy suggesting you'd water down your beer!'

'Ha ha ha!'

And they all laughed: 'HA! HA! HA!'

A brief sporting interlude

'Well with three tests rained off, England are in a better position than they could possibly have hoped for! And tonight, with nothing better to do, we are joined by Harold H. Ponsonby, captain of this once great, cricketing nation!

So,' he said turning to his guest of the evening. 'How was your journey from Ealing?'

'Not bad, not bad at all,' said the Captain. 'We took a while to get going, but once we did, the driver seemed to get into a groove and we fairly flew along!'

'Really?' said the interviewer, with a rapt, almost beatific expression on his face. 'Well now, let's talk about the cricket!'

The Captain nodded in agreement. It was a good plan. Although it was important to be flexible on these occasions.

'Well,' he said intensely. 'There hasn't actually been any cricket – on account of the rain.'

The Interviewer nodded sympathetically.

'But if things stay like this... we might even get a draw. Who knows? If we were really lucky we could even sneak a quick win at the Oval and then... well... that would go down in history as one of the great victories of our time! But it all depends on the weather. And the Australians.'

'Positive talk there from the English Captain!
And now, over to Jasper.'

The Ant-Heap

'Thank you,' said Jasper. 'Well this week we've come to *The Ant-Heap* which may look quiet now, but on a Saturday night is simply crawling with customers eager to sample the culinary delights prepared by innovative new chef, Jeff Slab.'

He turned to the stocky figure beside him.

'Good morning, Jeff!'

'Morning.'

'Now Jeff, I gather you used to be a rock-smasher in a quarry, is that right?'

'Yep.'

'And what was it that first sparked your interest in culinary matters, Jeff?'

'Hunger.'

Right!' smiled Jasper, and held the smile just a little too long. 'So, what are you preparing for us today?'

'Lapwing Pie,' he announced, sweeping off the lid in a grand gesture – the droplets of moisture, which had gathered on the underside of the lid, running off, dripping back into the pan. 'Mock-lapwing,' he added.

'So what is it then?'

'Chicken. Protected species lapwings, aren't they? Can't use them anymore.'

He clanged the lid back on the pan. 'Fancy a curlew roll?' he asked. 'Nice these – crunchy.'

Jasper winced at the sound of splintering beak.

'Dare I ask how you make them?' he asked.

'You may ask. But I couldn't tell you,' said Slab, flatly. 'I get'em from the Chinese, up the road.'

'Oh, I think we passed that on the way here,' said Jasper. 'Rather an old place with the dilapidated frontage?'

'What? Oh no, that's *The Jaded Empress*. You don't want to go there. You want *The Concubine's Pleasure Garden* – that's the place!'

'Full of mysterious allure, I should imagine.'

'Yeah,' said Slab. 'Loads of it.'

And still falls the rain…

The backdoor opened and Babbings came out at a run, holding a newspaper over his head. He ducked between the poles of the sagging *WELCOME!* banner, swerved between upturned tables and chairs, and reached the safety of the shed. He snatched open the door and dived inside.

Harry and Scabbit were playing another game of draughts with their upturned bottle tops, when Babbings burst in upon them.

'Have you seen what it says here?' He shook open the sodden paper, showering droplets in all directions. 'Ahem,' he began.

The two players looked up with the bored indifference of men who had spent the last four hours in a shed.

'Ahem,' said Babbings again. ' – here you read it.'

He handed the paper to Scabbit, who took it and shook it, and looked down at the headline.

'The Meteorological Office issued the following warning at 09.00

(oh nine-hundred hours) this morning,' he coughed, and looked up at his avid audience.

'If one more pint of rain falls today, this will officially become The Wettest Summer on Record since records began (in a somewhat genteel, amateurish way) in a Sussex garden in 1728.'

'What do you make of that, then?' asked Babbings triumphantly.

The rain was cascading past the serving hatch like the wrong side of a waterfall.

'Well I may not be an expert,' said Scabbit. 'But I'd say that's a lot more than a pint.'

'That's what I thought,' said Babbings, and he ran outside into the rain, head tipped back, the rain pouring on his face. 'Yes! Yes!' he punched the air and ran round in circles.

'What's erm… What's got into him do you think?' asked Harry.

'Not sure,' said Scabbit, scratching his head. 'Though I have seen him do something like that once before. It was another night in the Willesden Arena, and he was way down on points. And then in the thirteenth he came off the ropes…'

Babbings collects his winnings

It was all like a dream to him now. The way he had smacked the betting-slip down on the counter, Hartless trying to delude him into reinvesting in some hare-brained treble that paid 'way over the odds', Babbings remaining resolute, Hartless turning away, tasting the bitter gall of utter defeat, tapping the key that released the spring-loaded drawer of the till with it's many compartments, then shaking his head and reaching inside for the notes – the dirty bundle of grimy notes, and licking his fingers, counting them out as he laid them down on the counter. Glorious!

Babbings picked up his heap of winnings and stepped out into the rain.

The rain dripped from the peak of his sodden flat cap and ran down his face. The rain soaked through his shoes, making them soft and formless, as he splashed through the puddles. The rain was a cascading torrent splashing all around him. But the rain could not touch him.

He had done it! He had prised a wad of grimy notes off the bastard Hartless! He walked up the hill in the rain in a state of mystic euphoria. 'Yes!' he kept saying to himself. 'Yes!!' as he leapt and punched the air again.

A bus pulled alongside, held in the grip of the rain-slowed traffic. At its breath-blurred windows, faces stared blankly out. A woman with three kids and four shopping bags gawped vacantly at him.

'Look at that nut out there,' she said. ' – must be a looney.'

But Babbings was a holy fool who had known the cycle of despair and fortune. The wheel had turned full circle. The bus was pulling away.

With his wallet bursting and his pockets jangling, Babbings went off to celebrate in the only way he knew. He pushed open the door of the *Dog and Bucket*, and strode up to the counter leaving a trail of shiny wet footprints behind him.

'Don't often see you round this side,' said Allsop, dryly. 'Either you've got fed up of being in that shed of yours, or you've picked a winner.'

'Both!' said Babbings, in a good mood anyway, but secretly rather impressed by Allsop's perspicacity.

' – though what could be running in this miserable weather I don't know. It'd have to be a sea-horse!' He pulled back on the tap and the good ale hissed into the glass.

'How much did you win? If you don't mind me asking.'

'Enough,' replied Babbings, evasively.

Allsop went on twisting a white cloth inside a glass. Then he held it up and watched it gleam. He was a man who cared about his glasses, was Allsop, a man who took pride in his work. Fortune and despair didn't come into it.

'Old Hartless must be losing his touch,' said Allsop. 'Bet you wish you'd put more on now, eh? It's a sickener, isn't it? Always the way – put a lot on, you lose it – put a little, and you win. Life's like that.' He took down another glass, began twisting the white cloth inside it.

Babbings took another swallow of his beer. But the beer had begun to taste sour in his mouth, and he thought of his companions out in the leaky shed, with the rain beating on the roof, and the smell of burgers frying...

Yet another wasted journey

The Bentley glided away from the kerb, taking up its customary position astride the camber, the majestic wheels hissing over the slick-wet surface, the wipers going back and forth, back and forth. Gary Capstan, in his fine, gold-braided cap, was at the helm, Jasper and the Disembodied Voice were merely passengers.*

'Cheer up,' said the Disembodied Voice after they'd driven through five miles of rainy, suburban traffic. 'Here – have one of these boiled sweets.'

Jasper reached into the bag, his deft fingers scrabbling around amongst the contents and finally closing on one that had thought itself safe, hiding amongst the pack in the lower half of the bag. He pulled the two ends of the wrapper, the sweet turning over itself.

*F.E. – Ah yes – the pig-headed Gary Capstan – never knowingly passed on the open road. Former racing-driver, mechanic, spare-parts specialist. And now: chauffeur to those who can afford the time. His ambition is to drive a hearse. That way he could really create havoc on the roads.

He popped it in his mouth and looked out at the utter blandness of his surroundings: a row of shops, row of houses, row of shops, row of houses, post box... the awareness dawning upon him: 'Yuk! – this is a throat-lozenge!'

'That's right. I have them for my throat – for my *voice*, you understand.'

'Driver! Driver! Pull over!'

'Eh? What?' said Capstan, and in stretching up to look in the rear-view mirror, he inadvertently trod on the brake. The car bucked and jolted.

'Ooop!' came a voice from the back.

'What was that you said, Sir?'

'I've swallowed the bloody thing now!'

Capstan frowned, then raised his eyebrows enquiringly.

'Drive on.'

Capstan shrugged.

They drove on. In silence. Jasper looking out of his window, the Disembodied Voice looking out of his. But whereas Jasper was tight-lipped and morose, the Disembodied Voice was shaking, quivering with suppressed laughter.

Babbings gets cabin fever

Things had reached a critical phase. The rain was still falling, the garden was deserted, and Scabbit was still watching the rain.

'I wonder how far each one of those has fallen?' he said. 'Think of it – each raindrop falling alone through miles of sky...'

'Oh, my God,' said Babbings. 'I don't think I can take much more of this. I'm getting cabin fever.'

'Don't be silly you can't get cabin fever in a shed!' said Scabbit.

'Why not – log-cabin? Shed? What's the difference?'

'You don't catch it like that,' said Scabbit. 'You only get it when you're in a cabin on a boat, when you're cramped in a tiny space with nothing but four walls to stare at, and beyond, all around you, as far as the eye can see nothing but water... a vast expanse of water, a heaving... and all you can hear, and all you can see...'

'We're all in this together.'

"Stop! Stop! I'm going nuts!'

'Alright,' shrugged Scabbit. 'Only trying to help.'

For a while, all that could be heard was the sound of the rain.

'We could be here forever,' wailed Babbings. 'Maybe no one knows we're here anymore!'

'Things could be worse. At least we've got a roof over our heads,' said Scabbit. 'Something'll turn up. It always does.'

It did. A particularly violent squall struck the shed side on.

'Oh-oh! Even Noah's effin' Ark would capsize in this weather!' groaned Babbings.

For a moment it seemed that all was lost.

But Chippie Monkton was no amateur ark-builder. He knew a thing or two about carpentry, and the Shack, though rocked to its foundations, stood firm. The squall passed on in search of easier pickings – a loose fence-panel, or someone's chimney pot, perhaps.

Calm was restored.

'Sorry,' said Babbings, 'didn't mean to lose my rag. But this weather's getting on my nerves.'

'It's alright, Babbings,' said Scabbit. 'I know how you feel.'

'You do?' said the little man looking up, wanting so much to believe him.

Scabbit nodded. 'We're all in this together – don't you forget that, now.'

'I know,' said Harry. 'Let's play *I spy*. Go on Babbings, you can go first.'

'Oh, alright then. Thanks.'

He looked around him, the crisis had passed.

'I spy… with my little eye… something beginning with… R'

R is for Roof

That night as Dick Scabbit lay tossing and turning in his bed, sleeping the sleep of the just-but-somewhat-perturbed, he was woken by the splash of a raindrop bursting upon his creased and troubled brow. Another followed. And another. He blinked and sat up. The roof was leaking.

Dragging on his long black coat, which also served as a dressing gown, he positioned the ladder against the rim of the trapdoor that led to the attic, and began climbing the rungs. He folded back the trapdoor and breathed in the smell of the cold, dusty darkness. A scuffling noise came from somewhere under the eaves. He stood there, head and shoulders in the attic, blinking as his eyes grew accustomed to the dark. Before him was the dull grey loom of the water-tank with the huge round rivets in its side. He took in the problem at a glance – there was a gap between the slates where the rain was trickling through. But what he also took in, was a large chest standing bulkily just under the eaves.

This was clearly an omen. The mysterious machinations of the universe had brought him up here in the dead of night. He had long forgotten about this chest. It was an heirloom that had been in the Scabbit family for generations. But now, at last, its time had come. He tipped back the ancient, black wooden lid, and began rummaging around inside.

Some time later, hours or minutes who can tell? – for this was the dead of night, and Dick Scabbit had strayed into the timeless realms – a figure in a long black coat (and pyjamas) could be seen quietly descending the rungs of the ladder, carrying a large parcel wrapped in brown paper.

Now this was something that needed thinking about. And thinking required a good cup of tea. So off he went to the kitchen to prepare it. While the kettle was boiling he took another look at the strange package he had brought down.

The brown paper was crinkly and faded with age. And the string had been tied with a peculiar system of knotwork – intricate and confused at the same time – as if designed to deter all but the most determined seeker. A fact reaffirmed by the yellowed tag that he found attached: *Whosoever doth so open this – much wisdom will he find…*

He settled himself down on the sofa, took a satisfying sip of the tea and, resting the mug on the arm beside him, he set to work.

Old Grandmother Scabbit's book of secret recipes

The Common-Place Book of Isabella Scabbit including her own secret receipts for pickles, jams, conserves, and possets, and ointments and other remedyes of her own devising.

And that was a picture of her there in her bonnet, the only surviving picture of Old Grandmother Scabbit. It was a hard face and an old bonnet.

'Crikey – ugly old bird wasn't she?' thought Scabbit.

He felt a strange presence in the room, a sensation of pressure around the temples. For a moment it seemed that the eyes looking back at him had narrowed somewhat.

'Er... didn't mean it,' he said suddenly.

He took a hurried mouthful of tea to clear his head.

Dick Scabbit turned the stiff, and creaking pages, and drank of the strange wisdom within.

'A Salve for Canker of the Hoof.'

'Wild Tansy Souffle.'

'Steepwort Junket.'

He turned to the section entitled: *'Remedyes.'*

'For a case of bad humours smear mustard on the forehead and cover with a dock leaf, tie in place with a sheet of brown paper and lie very still in a darkened room.'

'There's a few people I'd like to try that on,' said Scabbit.

And while the rest of the world was sleeping, he thumbed through the stained and mildewed pages his ancestor had inscribed 'in her own fair hand.'

Possets

'What exactly is a posset?' he wondered. It was time to consult *The Big Dictionary of All Things*. He took it down from its shelf and flipped through the pages, mumbling to himself… *'Pike, Poke, Posset…*

Posset: a beverage of warm, curdled milk, sometimes flavoured with spices and brandy, often served to invalids and the bedridden.

Hmm... suppose they can't get away if they're bedridden.'

He closed the dictionary with a loud thump, and returned to Old Ma Scabbit.

His tea had gone cold, but he sipped at it anyway, so absorbed was he in the manuscript on his lap. Then he turned a page, and began to laugh...

'Old Ma Scabbit's Secret Relish.'

The rain had miraculously stopped. As if an unseen hand (gnarled and twisted with age) had turned off the stopcock. On roof and tile and leaf and branch, the rain had ceased to fall.

The Herald of a New Age

'Ha-ha!' he cried. 'Ha-ha!'

And after clattering about in the kitchen for an hour or so, he bounded up the stairs with the pan of relish in his hand.

'Harry wake up!'

By now it was daylight, or nearly so. The cold grey light of dawn filtered through the fibres of the curtain.

'Wake up! Wake up!'

Harry pushed himself up on one arm, felt on the top of the bedside cabinet for his glasses and hooked them over his ears.

'What time is it?' he asked sleepily.

'Time? Time? Who cares about time on a day like this!'

'Are you alright?' asked Harry.

'Me?' said Scabbit. 'I'm fine! Fine! Never better! Why do you ask?'

'What have you got in that pan? And why are you dressed in your pyjamas and an overcoat?'

Harry looked at his friend, and sighed. He knew he was in for a long day.

'Look! Look!' said Scabbit, and he swept back the curtains. In his exuberance a few curtain-hooks and those fiddly plastic ring-things pinged off in different directions.

'What am I looking at?' asked Harry who was surprisingly good-natured given the fact that he had just been roused from his sleep.

'The rain! The rain!'

'What rain?'

'Precisely! There *is* no rain! It's stopped! The waters have abated!'

Harry blinked, staring uncomprehendingly at the window. As he did so, a small bird, with a sharp beak and a forked tail, flittered down to perch on the window-ledge. The First Swallow, for it was he and none other, tapped on the glass. In his beak, he was holding a sprig of what looked like an olive branch. 'Here, forgot to give you this,' he seemed to say, and in a purring of wings he was gone.

'Oh my God I'm still dreaming,' said Harry pulling the covers back over his head.

'Harry, my boy. Our luck has changed!
I knew it would! I knew it! I knew it!
Ha! Ha! Ha! *The parched earth it drinketh rain...*'
But not anymore!
Our perilous quest is at an end! We have reached dry land!'

'What are you talking about?' asked Harry.

Storm-cloud reprise

The Matriarch gathered her storm clouds about her.

Her voice rang out through the desolate heavens. 'Our work here is done. Our purpose is served. We have done what we came here to do!'

That brought a rumble of appreciation, and a few flashy lightning strikes from the more extrovert members.

'There is no sense hanging around,' she continued.

'Where next?' 'Where to now?' they all wanted to know.

'Patience, my people, patience,' she said. 'I was just coming to that.'

'So the old girl's not senile, yet,' said a wisp from the fringes of the vortex.

The Matriarch resumed, but took note.

'Let's nip across the Channel for a quick spree!'

'Oh goody,' said a middle-aged cumulus to her neighbour. 'I've always rather fancied Le Touquet!'

They resumed formation and drifted away.

Fine weather at last

The Weatherman was in sullen mood. Too bad-tempered even to extemporise upon the script he had been given.

'The Met Office issued the following warning at 09.00 hours this morning,' he read listlessly. *'The entire country is basking in fine weather. There is not a single cloud within five hundred miles of this island (except for the one over the power-station at Didcot). This situation is likely to continue for the foreseeable future. We will give you an update as soon as we have anything miserable to report.'*

He painstakingly removed the clouds from the map behind him. Then turned to face the camera.

'Still not as nice the Seychelles,' he said.

*

At 14.00 hours there was an update.

'Ha! Got it!' said the Weatherman tearing the paper from the printer.

Moments later he was on the air, behind him a scorched and barren map. Sun everywhere, pitiless and blinding to the eye.

'The Met Office has issued drought warnings throughout the land!' he said almost frothing at the mouth in his excitement. 'There will be drought, plagues, pestilence...All coming your way! Bet you wish you'd left out a few buckets when it was raining, eh? Too late now! Ha! A drought has been declared with a hosepipe-ban to be enforced by local busybodies, dog-walkers, and strange men with clipboards. So, you may be happy sitting out there in your garden. But it won't last! Your lawn's going to shrivel!'

His self-satisfied smile faded into oblivion.

Business at the Food Shack was brisk

'Like a little bit of relish on that, sir?' asked Scabbit.

'Ooh no, no, no. I don't like relish!' said a timid customer.

'Ah, but you'll like *this* relish.'

'No, no, really I don't – I can't stand the stuff.'

'Ah, go on. Try it. Just a dollop!' And he applied a large dollop of relish and closed the bun firmly.

'I tell you what,' said Scabbit. 'If you don't like it, you can throw it over the hedge and I'll give you another one.'

'Without relish?'

'If that's what you want.'

'Which hedge?'

'Er... make it the nine-footer across the street,' said Scabbit, just to be on the safe side.

Very tentatively, the timid customer bit into the burger.

A smile spread over his face. Over both of their faces.

'But this is not relish! This is… this is…' he took another bite. 'It can't be.'

'Relish,' said Scabbit, nodding.

'You mean all these years I've been avoiding relish and missing out on… on this?'

'Afraid so. How old are you?'

'Sixty-seven.'

'Sixty-seven? Sixty-seven years without relish? You poor man. Still, probably got a couple of years left in you. As long as you don't overdo it. Next!'

Ride with the wind

Jasper, meanwhile, was returning from yet another fruitless visit, this time to *Turpins!* a coaching inn on the Great North Road. *Now serving simple hearty fare for the traveller with a long ride ahead of him, and the wind behind.* He had just sampled *Black Bess's Treat – a traditional heavy-set suet pudding embedded with currants and liberally plastered with custard.* It was filling fare. The kind that may have been good coming out of a nosebag (except for the custard) after a brisk gallop on a cold day with the frost glinting on the trees, and your hooves ringing sparks from the frozen road. But on a breathless August afternoon, it was just not the same.

*

It was a hot day and Jasper was parched. Hotter than he could ever remember, and in need of immediate liquid refreshment, as was the radiator of the Bentley in which he was being driven. In fact at that very moment, its unsatisfying mixture of stale, rust-tinged water with added rusty bits floating in it, was bubbling beneath its flimsy 'screw tight but do not over-tighten' lid and adding to the compression within its already sorely-perished rubber hoses.

With a final, suffocating effort, the water surged upward, forced apart the fibres of the hose and erupted in clouds of hissing steam.

There! – it bubbled happily all down the engine block.

The release was wonderful!

It hissed contentedly. Well that was that, for a while.

'What the...?' said Gary Capstan, his vision somewhat clouded. He swerved into the side of the kerb, narrowly missing a man on a bicycle who gripped the handlebars and bounced up onto the pavement with a genial: 'Look where you're going, mate!' accompanied by a quaint old gesture handed down from the archers of Agincourt, before ploughing headlong into the privet.

'That's torn it,' said the Disembodied Voice, raising his eyebrows.

In due course, Capstan got out, exchanged pleasantries with the cyclist – bidding him be on his way *or he'd have more than a wobbly front-wheel to worry about, the ponce* – flipped up the lid of the bonnet and began wafting ineffectually at the clouds of steam with his rather smart gold-braided cap.

'I recall being stranded once,' began the Disembodied Voice, who had come round the front to see what was happening. 'On that occasion we were able to effect a temporary repair with the aid of my companion's nylon stockings which served as a makeshift fan belt.'

'Yeah, well can't help you there,' said Capstan. 'Anyway this ain't the bleedin' fan belt, it's the bleedin' 'ose what's gone and bust itself.'

'I was merely reminiscing,' said the Disembodied Voice.

'This is no good,' said Gary Capstan. 'I'm going for help,' and he went round to the back of the car and took out a large red triangle.

'How does that work exactly?' asked Jasper.

'Is it perhaps some kind of signalling device?' asked the Disembodied Voice.

'Look, why don't you two leave this to me?' said Capstan.

The Parched Earth

After about four hundred yards of scorching, featureless, suburban pavement they came to a little gate…

'What's that?' said Jasper.

'Looks like a gate, to me,' said the Disembodied Voice, astutely.

'Of course it's a gate! I know it's a gate. What I mean is: what's behind it?'

'Well let's find out,' said the Voice, and he pushed open the gate and went inside. As they walked along the path, the sounds of raised-glasses, and laughter, and alcohol-assisted camaraderie, reached their ears. Suddenly, there in front of them was a drooping, tatty banner sagging between two poles. The letters had run and the cloth was faded – but the meaning was clear: *WELCOME*!

'That's more like it!' said the Disembodied Voice.

And stepping beneath the banner, they found themselves in a little garden.

'Welcome friends! I bid you welcome!' said a strange long-haired figure, manically snatching up glasses and plates and then wiping the table with his sleeve. '*The parched earth it drinketh rain...* but you might prefer a beer!' he said. 'Bar's over there. We do the food!' And with that he hurried off across the garden.

'I tell you what,' said Jasper. 'I'll sit down over here and have a little rest while you go and fetch the drinks. I am parched,' he declared, looking around him. 'Parched.'

And the good people of the neighbourhood were happy...

Ice cold in a tall glass

The Disembodied Voice returned, carrying two tall, straight glasses with some cryptic Danish script on the front of them. The beer was cold and the glasses were beaded with condensation. Jasper raised the glass to his eye-level, and looked at that cool clear fluid within. He swallowed a couple of times in anticipation. 'Well I don't know about you, but all this travelling back and forth across the country has made me very thirsty.'

'Bottoms up,' said the Disembodied Voice.

But Jasper was savouring the moment. He drew his finger down the side of the glass, tracing a clear line through the droplets of condensation. Then he brought the glass to his lips and drank. And drank. And drank.

'Ahhh…' he said setting down the empty glass. 'Fill'em up again, will you?'

'Me?' said the Disembodied Voice. 'But it's your turn! I got the last one!'

Jasper sighed, and went off to the bar.

He made his way up to a strangely-cut stable door, from behind which Allsop the barman was dispensing a choice of three fine local ales: *Drayhorse's Kick, Old Plodder, Knacker's Kneecap*, and a guest ale, *Sopwith's Summer Ale*. Jasper perused the heraldic devices on the front of the taps.

'What's the *Drayhorse's Kick* like?

'A bit of a surprise if you're not used to it.'

'Hmmm. Two pints of *Sopwith's Summer Ale*, then please,' he said.

'Probably wise,' said Allsop the barman. 'The other's more of a winter ale, really.'

Jasper watched keenly as Allsop went about his time-honoured craft. As a great artist himself, he knew he was in the presence of a master. He was particularly impressed when Allsop took up a convenient palette knife and cut off the excess foam. Now *that* was attention to detail. Jasper nodded in approval.

Allsop handed the two beautifully-drawn pints of golden ale across the serving hatch.

'Right, there you go. And mind out for that unexpected dip in the grass over there. There's a few come a cropper on that already. Complete waste of good ale. Right, who's next?'

The Fan

In no time at all, Jasper and the Disembodied Voice were sitting contentedly – that first rapacious thirst having been satisfied – sipping at their replenished glasses. It was a warm and peaceful summer's afternoon, and the good people of the neighbourhood were happy and relaxed, stealing a few hours of freedom from the toil of the daily grind. They sat at their tables, chatting, drinking, engaged in conversation with themselves and each other. For these were simple folk, and good at heart. Jasper found himself warming to them. He smiled and looked out at the scene around him with a kindly eye.

'Ere! I think I know you,' said a voice suddenly close at hand.

'So do I – but I always surprise myself!' said Jasper.

'No, not you. *Him*,' said the Fan, jabbing a thumb in the direction of the Disembodied Voice.

'*Him?*'

'It is you isn't it? Go on! Say something!'

Jasper frowned. But the Disembodied Voice smiled modestly.

'Hel-lo,' he said, displaying, in those two long drawn-out syllables, the full range of his perfectly-modulated voice.

'I knew it! It is you! You're the voice what talks on his show. The one who keeps interrupting! I love it when you do that! He gets so narked off! Ha! Ha! Ha! I thought I recognised you!'

Jasper looked down at his glass, he swirled the beer around, but somehow didn't feel like drinking any of it. His good humour was evaporating. In fact, he was feeling decidedly 'narked off.'

'I was just saying to my friend over there, I've heard you many times on the television of course, saying things like: 'And now for the omelette,' and 'What are you doing with that egg exactly?' – that was a good one! But I never thought I'd ever actually get to hear you with my own ears, face to face as we are now! It's a honour. A great honour!'

The Disembodied Voice blushed, smiling behind his spectacles.

'You're not a bit like I imagined you though. With a voice like that I thought you'd be a big strong feller. Not a weedy little bloke!'

'Oh,' said the Voice. 'Everyone says that.'

'Well, see you around!' Their visitor beamed and tottered off, pint in hand.

Jasper smiled contentedly and drained his glass, tipping it up, so as to allow the last flavoursome droplets to settle upon his discerning taste buds. His good humour once again restored.

'Very nice, this *Summer Ale*,' he said. 'A fine choice!'

'Right,' said the Disembodied Voice. 'Well, I think I'll go for a little wander.'

A Voice in the Wilderness

The smoke from the barbecue was wafting pleasantly across the summer's evening, stinging the eyes, and obscuring the subtler scents of jasmine and evening honeysuckle. The Disembodied Voice inhaled peacefully, and immediately regretted it.

'Drink,' he gasped, clutching his throat, as he stumbled up to the serving hatch. 'My voice! Got to have a drink…'

'Wait your turn, mate!' said a friendly local. 'Pint of *Summer Ale*, please!' he said turning to Allsop the barman.

Allsop nodded, reached for a glass and pulled back on the tap. The fine golden ale hissed, frothing, into the angled glass and, with each pull of the tap, the level rose.

'What's the matter with him?' asked Allsop.

'Oh just the old choking gag,' said the local. And then turning to the Disembodied Voice: 'We've all tried it mate, but Old Allsop's not going to fall for a trick like that.'

Allsop shook his head and pursed his lips emphatically.

'But you don't understand! I'll ruin my voice… My voice is everything to me!'

'Yeah, well there's a few people seem to think like that.'

The Big Green Bus

Just then a big green bus pulled up, and eleven men wearing green blazers and baggy green caps jumped down into the street.

They paused beneath the *WELCOME!* banner.

'Is that for us, Skip?'

'Yeah, must be I suppose.'

Then he stood before his men and eyed them sternly. 'Now remember, I want you on your best behaviour tonight, OK? And if you must play games with the Pommies, you know: cards, shove-halfpenny, darts, whatever – at least let'em win sometimes, alright?'

He paused with his hand on the top of the little gate.

'And another thing. The first round's on me. After that you're on your own.'

'Yay!' 'Good old Skip!' 'Yaaaaay!'

'Alright, that'll do. I don't want you to like me. I just want you to follow me.'

'It's alright Skip, we don't like you!'

'OK that's enough, now follow me.'

They did. Right up to Allsop's serving hatch.

'Evening, mate!' said Skip, leaning a green-blazered elbow on the serving hatch.

'Good evening,' nodded Allsop, warily.

Skip glanced quickly at the taps and reached an instant decision: 'Eleven pints of *Drayhorse's Kick*.'

Allsop sniffed. 'That's more of a Winter Ale, really.'

'Yeah, well it's our winter isn't it?'

'Your winter?'

Birds of a feather

High above them, The First Swallow was heading south, it's small feathered crop bulging with mosquitoes, fat crunchy horseflies, and various succulent snacks for the journey ahead. It looked down on the Riviera, its little wings flittering easily in that warm sunlight.

*

Meanwhile, up over Le Touquet (and therefore some way behind the fast-moving swallow) the Matriarch and her stalwart thunderclouds were letting them have it. Their approach had been magnificent. Graceful and menacing in its apparent slowness. The formation had appeared in mid-afternoon – a thin dark line on the far horizon. Moments later the beach was in disarray. A tangle of upturned deckchairs and brightly coloured umbrellas scattered as the panicked bathers snatched up what belongings they could – a pair of sunglasses, canvas shoulder bag, fat dog-eared book, large sandy towel with faded starfish motif on the front, sandals, suntan lotion, bucket and spade, 'Oups!' – small wailing child, and ran up the beach.

By now the rain was lashing down, lightning cracked the sky (and thunder too, a fraction of a second later – for the storm was almost directly overhead) and the bedraggled bathers were huddling beneath the flapping awnings of shopfronts (selling sunglasses, canvas shoulder bags, suntan lotion etc.) while the rain splashed and bounced all around them.

Back in the garden

The men in the baggy green caps and blazers stood around the fringe of a scythe-slashed herbaceous border, politely supping their pints.

'Are you the Australians?' said the Fan. 'I knew it! I knew it! I was just saying to my friend over there…'

'Yep.'

'Any chance of a team picture?'

'Sure,' said the Captain, eager for any good publicity that might come his way. For he saw himself not just as a sporting icon, but as an ambassador for left-handers everywhere.

'Right men, drink up! We're having a team photo. Put your glasses down over there. Shorty you come down here at the front.'

'Oh Ski-ip! I'm always at the front!'

'Just – that'll do. Ready? Right.'

And two neat lines of men in green blazers (very smart) and caps were lined up in front of the flowerbed, smiling pleasantly.

The Fan stood facing them, pint in hand, smiling back.

The seconds lingered.

It was the Captain who realised something was amiss. 'Where's your camera?' he asked.

'I haven't got a camera,' said the Fan shaking his head. 'That's why I asked for a team picture. I thought you carried them around with you in those blazers. Must have lots of pockets in a thing like that.'

'Alright men,' sighed the Captain. 'Back to your beer.'

'But we gulped it all down.'

'Yeah I've got the burbles now Skip.'

'Yeah – you told us to drink it all up and we did.'

'Alright, alright. I'll get this round but that's the last one alright? After that you're on your own.'

'Yay!' 'Good old Skip!' 'Yaaaaay!'

'Alright – I don't want you to like me.'

They followed him up to Allsop's serving hatch.

'Back already?' said Allsop, frowning. 'Shouldn't rush a good ale, you know. That's why we get'em delivered by horse and cart. Two lovely old shire horses bring them with big furry feet.'

'*Knackers* – eleven pints of *Knackers*.'

Journey's End

Jasper took a drink from his foam-stained glass. Above him, the birds were flitting back and forth, and from other parts of the garden came laughter and snatches of conversation. The afternoon was sliding inexorably into evening and Jasper was now beginning to feel slightly peckish. Over in the far corner of the garden was a peculiar shed, with a black stovepipe sticking out of the roof. He walked towards it, sniffing appreciatively at the aroma of sizzling onions.

'I am famished,' he declared as he approached the shed. 'Famished.'

'Then you've come to the right place, my friend! Here, try one of these.' And he was handed some kind of burger, in a flour-dusted bap.

'Thank you,' said Jasper.

Absent-mindedly he took a bite out of the burger, and swilled it down with some more of the beer. He took another bite, staring blankly at his surroundings... a garden filled with the sounds of drinking, and raucous laughter... the scent of evening-honeysuckle trailing on the breeze, the odours of traffic pollution, and the tang of barbecue smoke. People sat at tables. People, nameless faces. The side of his tongue became aware of a subtle... a delicious hint of... what was it?

Old Ma Scabbit's relish was what it was.

'But this... But this...'

And slowly the light began to dawn.

His quest was at an end.

'But this is no ordinary burger – actually it's a very ordinary burger – but the relish, the relish...' he exclaimed.

'Tasty isn't it!' grinned the face from the serving hatch.

'Show me the man who made this wondrous...'

'I did,' said Scabbit.

'You??'

Jasper takes the stage

Jasper climbed up on to the roof of the Shack and spread wide his arms.

The drunks jeered appreciatively – the entertainment was beginning.

'I'm sure you all know who I am…'

'Nope.'

Jasper cackled good-naturedly. 'I am Jasper Watson – star of the ever-popular *Wats-on the Plate?*'

'It's him! It's him! It's Jasper Watson!'

'I've got all of his knives,' said a quiet voice.

'And I'm sure you're probably wondering what I'm doing here, standing on top of this… shed?'

'Nope.'

'Happens all the time round here, mate!'

'Skip! Sk-ip!'

'No idea,' said the man in the green cap. 'Must be some new kind of Pommie game… Just wait a minute while I figure it out.'

'Well today is a very special day!' said the man on the roof.

'Oh, Mickey,' said a piercing, feminine voice. 'Is this another of those comedians you've hired?'

'Nothing to do with me, love.'

'Well at least he's got their attention, I suppose, which is more than the last one did.'

And he had. For they were used to the drunks performing but it was never usually allowed to go this far.

'As I'm sure you all know, over the last few months …'

'Nope!'

'Ha! Ha!' he laughed.

'Ha! Ha!' they laughed back.

'Over the last few months, we have travelled the length and the breadth of the land.'

He spread his arms wide again, to show just how wide the land was.

'As you know the competition this year was particularly hot, particularly... fierce.'

He paused for them to finish nodding their heads.

'Hot and fierce,' he said again, in case they hadn't been following. 'But today our journey is at an end! And it gives me great pleasure... to announce the *winner* of this year's *Chef of Distinction!* He paused for effect:

'This year's *Chef of Distinction!*' shouted Jasper, 'is none other than the proprietor of the Food Shack – your very own... DICK... SCABBIT!'

The applause was deafening.

Scabbit smiled at them, as he was presented with a *Smilers' Slicer* with a gold-plated hilt, a nice red sash, and a framed certificate with his name in fancy writing.

'I shall treasure these trappings of success,' he said proudly.

Dick Scabbit: *Chef of Distinction!*

'Now of course, we need to film you actually making this most excellent relish,' the Director explained.

'Of course,' said Scabbit. 'Why's that, then?'

'Why? For posterity, of course!'

'Posterity?'

'Yes.'

'So it's not just some cheap, voyeuristic form of entertainment?'

'Oooh no!' frowned the Director, horrified.

*

Harry and Scabbit were just finishing a late breakfast when the sedate form of the Bentley drew up outside.

'Ah good morning!' said Jasper.

He and the Disembodied Voice stamped their feet on the doormat and trailed along the corridor into the kitchen.

'Well, this is the kitchen!' said Scabbit, and gestured around him, as if it were a far larger room than in fact it was.

The doorbell rang again.

'That'll be the Crew,' said Jasper.

And in they came. The sound-man with his silver boxes, the lighting-man with his silver boxes and big silver umbrellas, the cameraman with his camera... Soon the hallway, the front room, and part of the staircase were blocked with heaps of expensive equipment. Then came the cables. Miles and miles of thick black cables, snaking in and out of the kitchen, looping up the stairs and trailing back along the hallway to the front room, where a man in a black baseball cap began plugging the ends into a large black box. This was clearly the nerve-centre of the entire operation.

Harry and Scabbit watched with interest as the place filled up around them.

'Lucky we got here early,' said Harry. ' – might not have got a seat otherwise.'

'Ha!' said Scabbit, and leaning back in his chair he rested his feet on a black box containing some priceless piece of equipment. 'Just the right height,' he said.

The man with the big silver umbrellas began opening them up.

'What are those for then, mate?' asked Scabbit.

'Reflectors.'

'Oh – reflectors.'

'Right who's got my chair,' said the Director. 'It's got my name on the back. Anyone seen it?'

'It's here,' said his sylphlike assistant, Emily. 'I was just dragging it into position.'

'Hmmm, well put it over there next to the door. Not too near – I don't want to be caught in a cross-draught.'

The preparations were complete. Or almost complete. The make-up girl with very long eyelashes approached Jasper and began patting his face with a large pink powder puff. She took a step towards Dick Scabbit who backed away. 'No – thought not,' she laughed.

Everyone was at their posts. Alert and focussed. Someone coughed.

'Right. Let's roll,' said the Director.

Jasper stood confidently in front of the camera. Emily stepped forward with her clapperboard and clacked it shut. 'Action!' she said.

'I've always wanted to do that,' said Scabbit. 'Have you ever shut your fingers in it?'

There were groans from the entire crew.

'Right, Take Two,' sighed the Director. 'Try not to talk unless you're spoken to, please Mr Scabbit.'

Scabbit turned his head slowly and raised an eyebrow. Harry laughed in the background. But the crew were deep in concentration, their faces tense with the seriousness of the moment.

Emily stepped forward with her clapperboard again. 'Take Two and... Action!' She clacked it, and withdrew gracefully to one side.

'Hello and welcome to *Wats-on the Plate?*' said Jasper, hurriedly.

'Well today we join Mr Dick Scabbit – this year's *Chef of Distinction!* who is going to prepare for us a very special recipe. Perhaps you'd like to tell us what you're preparing for us today, Mr Scabbit?'

'Old Ma Scabbit's Relish.'

'That's right,' said Jasper. '*Old Ma Scabbit's Relish.* And I have to say it is the most delicious relish I have ever tasted. I'm sure everyone at home simply can't wait for you to show us how it is made! Over to you Mr Scabbit.'

'Thanks,' said Scabbit, picking up an onion. 'Well first you take an onion. An ordinary onion – like this,' and he held it up, turning it round in his hand, as if it were a quite extraordinary onion.

'Was that OK?' he asked.

'Very good,' the Disembodied Voice reassured him. 'I think you have the gift, Mr Scabbit. The gift.'

'Thank you,' nodded Scabbit, and picked up the knife which had been provided for him. 'Funny knife,' he said, turning it so it caught the light.

'Ah, yes,' said Jasper interrupting. 'That is *The Smiler Flenser* – one of my very own cluster of knives, made for me specially by *Smilers of Sheffield. Forged in steel, crafted in Sheffield! Nothing cuts like a Smiler!*'

'Is that right?' said Scabbit. 'Well anyway, you take your onion, and you slice it up, like this.' Slowly and firmly he sawed his way through the onion, then wiped his hands on his shirt-front. 'Then you pop it in the pan, like this.'

'Is there a special way of doing that?' asked the Disembodied Voice.

'No.'

'Oh, how refreshing,' sighed the Disembodied Voice.

'Then in go your apples…'

Scabbit reached for a wooden spoon and began to stir.

There was a sudden commotion as Jasper made his way into the edge of the frame. 'Wait, wait, wait! What's that you've got there?'

'It's a spoon,' frowned Scabbit. 'One of my very own Scabbit Spoons – this one is called *The Scoop!*'

'Well our viewers might like to know about that.'

Scabbit looked at the viewers in disbelief.

Then, shaking his head, he got on with his stirring. 'I am now stirring the pot,' he said. 'With *The Scoop*.'

For once, even the Disembodied Voice was silent. Scabbit tipped in half a bowl of brown sugar without further comment.

'Excuse me just a minute,' said Jasper, stepping carefully over the thick black cables. 'I just need to have a few words with the Director.

Scabbit turned once more to the bubbling pan. He stirred it slowly, gently, becoming mesmerised by the bubbles breaking on its surface, by the swirls of colour – like the continents of some youthful universe – melding, shifting, coalescing…

'Now the secret…'

'This is it now,' hissed Jasper excitedly in the adjoining room.

'The secret which makes this different from all other relishes, or chutneys or pickles or ketchups come to that…'

'Come on! Come on!' muttered Jasper impatiently. 'Get on with it! Are we recording OK? Is everything OK?'

The sound-man looked up from his box of dials and flickering level indicators, and nodded slowly.

'The secret…' said Scabbit, and at that point a bubble burst and a drop of the scalding hot relish splashed onto his thumb. 'Ouch!' he exclaimed, and stuck his thumb in his mouth to quench the pain. As he did so, the mysterious flavours of *Old Ma Scabbit's Relish* broke upon his taste buds and he felt himself transported to another realm. A realm of light and kindness, of wisdom, and infinite understanding. A realm where his thumb did not throb with pain, and his kitchen wasn't crowded with a film-crew and yet, this strange and beautiful world was not so very far away from our own – for there below him was the roof of the house, where the sun was shining on the broken tiles.

He floated for a while in the warm summer air, looking out over the roofs of the city where he lived. In the distance he could see a little garden with a ramshackle shed in it, and beyond that, the railway line where a train was passing, and beyond that, further still, was the curve of the Great River where the swirls in the current showed that even as he watched, the tide was beginning to turn.

A strange rippling sensation came over him, and he passed through the roof, through tile and beam. He could see all within – see all, and hear all too. And in one of the rooms he saw Jasper crouched over the flickering screen of a monitor. 'Come on!' he heard him say. 'Come on! Tell me the secret! I *must* have the secret!'

And Scabbit realised then that he had been tricked, lured by the glamour of shiny things… Then the pain seared up at him, and there he was, back in the kitchen, stirring a pan with a wooden spoon. Jasper came bursting into the kitchen with the Director hot on his heels.

'But what about the secret? You haven't told us the secret?'

'You know, I think perhaps I'll keep that to myself,' said Scabbit.

And the vision came to him then, of a vast and hallowed emporium where all the finest foods were sold. And on shelf, after shelf, and on jar after jar, Old Ma Scabbit's face scowled back at him – with her beaky nose and dirty old bonnet.

Though now perhaps, there *was* a glint in her eye.

The End.

You have been watching:

(All characters are caught in likely poses and will smile pleasantly as the camera lingers upon them.)

Mickey Jakes – the landlord of the *Dog and Bucket* standing with his hands on his hips surveying his bustling new beer garden on a summer's eve. The birds are singing, the good folk are laughing, and a train goes past in the distance.

And there's Allsop the barman – on duty behind his newly-cut stable door. An eager throng, holding up their empty glasses, jostling for his attention. 'Right, who's next?'

Chippie Monkton – gentleman-carpenter, builder of the Food Shack. There he is look, hammering away at the side of the shed – just a few final touches, eh Chippie?

And here's Mandy Jakes – wife of landlord Jakes. A kindly, woman with an excruciating laugh. There she is with a basket of goodies for the shed-dwellers. Hello Mandy!

Ah, and there's The Weatherman – no smile there I'm afraid. What an extraordinary jacket. The camera begins to ripple out of focus… Not surprised. Who's next?

Why it's Jasper Watson! – star of the ever-popular *Wats-on the Plate?* Here we see him in typical pose, hunched over his chopping board. Look at that silver-blue blur of Sheffield steel. Now that is the way to chop an onion!

The knife, of course, has been provided by *Smilers of Sheffield*. *Smilers* are known for their catchy advertising slogans: '*Nothing cuts like a Smiler.*' '*If you can't hack it – use a Smiler!*' and the jaunty '*Rare blades and true, handcrafted for you-hoo.*' etc.

And now the camera sweeps up into the blue of a summer sky, where a small bird is seen flittering... there he goes look: The First Swallow – heading south to warmer climes!

And higher still… The Matriarch – a large cloud, drifting along slowly at the head of her herd.

And above them all, watching with unforgiving gaze…

Isabella Scabbit – known as 'Old Ma Scabbit' on account of her age, and wisdom. Generally pictured, as here, in black and white – wearing her distinctive dirty old bonnet.

Epilogue:

Freak Weather Front Hits Seychelles!

The Seychelles have been hit by the most peculiar weather front in the islands' history. Days and days of low-cloud, and cold, lingering drizzle. Drizzle! – in the Seychelles! We simply can't understand it,' say experts. (Honest for once.) 'Nor can we!' say the islanders. 'We're used to sudden tropical storms, hurricanes, bending palm trees… but this is getting us down. We haven't seen the sun for weeks now. The coconut monkeys have stopped being mischievous and are just sitting around in sad little clumps (the trunks of the palm trees are too slippery for them to climb). Even the parrots have stopped talking. Not that they said anything interesting anyway. But now they've stopped we miss them.'

'Ah,' sighed the Matriarch. 'This is the life! I'd always dreamed of retiring somewhere like this. So peaceful. So little to do… Yes, I think I'll be staying here for quite some time…

Goodbye, my loves. Goodbye.'

And the herd swirled past her for the very last time, a few of them shedding the odd minor downpour, and she watched them drift slowly out over the horizon.

Wispy Gorman – a few autobiographical details.

Birth / The Early Years – this period is dealt with in more detail in the highly entertaining *Wispy Gorman – the autobiography*. Was nicknamed 'Wispy' on account of his being a thin, undernourished child. Even the loyal family doctor once commented: 'My God! Look at those ribs – don't they feed you at home?' This upset the young Gorman who was already developing into a withdrawn, sensitive child. Mrs Gorman wasn't too happy about it either. *The World of Work*. Heeding the good doctor's advice, Wispy took a job that would bring him close to plentiful supplies of food. He enlisted as a humble kitchen-boy in an establishment not dissimilar to the *Dog and Bucket*. But the long hours working alongside unstable men with sharp knives took their toll. And Wispy decided to leave, having hidden in the walk-in deep freeze long enough to devour an entire chocolate cake. He emerged feeling cold, and slightly sick. And with his hair as stiff as a brush. It was time to move on. Somewhere warmer. *The Spanish Years*. These were happy, carefree years and Wispy began writing poetry. '*Oh Luna! Luna!*' etc. After a few years he returned with an old, beech-framed trunk bulging with poems. He lived in an attic in Lambeth enduring all kinds of hardship and poverty in pursuit of his art. It is this period of 13 years which inspired and informed *The Wispy Gorman Stories*.

The Wispy Gorman Stories:

Harry Hop-Pole

Chef of Distinction!

The Ray of Truth

Dick Scabbit and the Reindeer

The Finger of Destiny

The End of the World.

A short extract from the next Wispy Gorman story:
The Ray of Truth

The smoke curled and disappeared. It was expensive smoke, but that didn't bother Mr Leonidas. For Mr Leonidas was a very rich man. And on top of that he had just completed a most satisfactory purchase. A painting. There it was on the floor in front of him, leaning against the leg of a divan. The frame was gilded and somewhat overdone, though at present, its lower edge was obscured by the white tufts of a Persian rug. It was a painting of a pond. And Mr Leonidas was staring at it intently. It was said there was mystery within its depths, and Mr Leonidas was a collector of mysteries. He watched and he waited. In time all mysteries would be revealed. He puffed again on the thin black cheroot. The smoke curled and disappeared.

Hmmm – intriguing, eh? I wonder what that's all about? Find out in the next instalment! – F.E.

SPECIAL OFFER

For the first time, the entire *Smilers* range of very sharp knives is now available in a limited edition box set. Do not delay! This offer is only available while stocks last. (We have a small aircraft hangar stacked to the rafters, and once that's empty that really is it. There will be no more.)

Each knife has been handcrafted by loving craftsmen. We use only the finest carbon steel which is bashed on the anvil by Wedgewood Clunk the Blacksmith, before being ground to spark-splintering sharpness by Sydney Silverman (Knife-grinder).

And now...

'We go live to Mr Sydney Silverman, the old knife-grinder.

Well Mr Silverman perhaps you'd tell us a little bit about your craft – about how you began, your apprenticeship, all those years at the grindstone, the beginnings of the automated age, the future of knife-grinding...

Over to you Mr Silverman!'

'Brrrrrrr! Brrrr! Brrrr! – that'll be ninepence.'

acorn book company

is an independent
publisher of small, high quality editions.

For more information
please visit us at:
www.acornbook.co.uk

'Don't do that you Old Fool – you'll ruin it!'

'I been grinding knives since…'

'But those are my house keys?'